T0128835

Just a Simple Job

Earle W. Jacobs

authorHOUSE®

AuthorHouse™
1663 Liberty Drive
Bloomington, IN 47403
www.authorhouse.com
Phone: 1-800-839-8640

First published by AuthorHouse 6/29/2011

ISBN: 978-1-4634-1290-6 (e)
ISBN: 978-1-4634-1291-3 (hc)
ISBN: 978-1-4634-1292-0 (sc)

Library of Congress Control Number: 2011909145

Printed in the United States of America

Part One

One Thing Just Lead to Another

(This is a sequel to '"Good Heavens, Miss Evans!")

CHAPTER ONE

GRETHEL HAD SO MUCH fun in Las Vegas I almost could not pry her away. It was even worse when we got to Disneyland. I think she is a frustrated Mouseketeer. Of course, she had read of these places but the reality of them for someone who had not been outside Europe for many years was truly a revelation. Of course, it was fun for me also seeing these with someone who had not ever been anywhere like these places. "You know, my dear William," she told me, "I do think this must be one of the best honeymoons I have ever been on! You really are a very dear husband." She now kids me as much as I do her.

She surely does not look like she is over four months pregnant. I have been asking her if she was sure about this condition, she professes to have. Using a whiney, quavering voice, I ask her if she is just claiming to be pregnant so she could force me to marry her. Her usual reply was that in the event I did not accomplish that when we were on top of the mountain I most assuredly would have by now, considering my more recent heroic endeavors. My, my, she does have a way with words, doesn't she?

She likes the kidding around that we do. She says there had never been much humor in her life up to now. She hadn't realized how dull her life had been all those years. In my family, I told her, it had been just the opposite of that. I guess that is why I had such a happy childhood.

Chapter Two

WE ARE TEMPORARILY BACK in our old motel room. My furniture and household goods from my place down south are in storage in a big moving van parked here in town. I get to pay rent on that until we have a place to put things. My house down there is in the hands of a Property Manager and will be rented for the time being. I should do all right on that, rentals being what they are right now.

Elaine is fond of repeating, always within my hearing of course, that it was imperative that she and Grethel find something big enough to house all my *numerous* progeny. I keep telling them that what they heard was the word humorous. They both maintain however that they both clearly heard me say, "Numerous." I tell them it is not fair when they are ganging up on me two against one. Anyway, the girls are having a lot of fun checking out the available real estate. I hope we can come up with something soon. The rental on that big van is getting pretty expensive.

It surely is nice now to see Grethel so happy and contented----most of the time. I have noticed that at times, when she doesn't know anyone is watching, she will gaze off into space with a pensive look on her face. I suspect I know what causes that and I am waiting for the right time to talk to her about it. I hate however to break the happy spell she seems to be under right now.

CHAPTER THREE

WELL, A DECISION HAS been made; we are going to rent a three bedroom, bath and three-quarter, ranch style house until next year. The ladies in the meantime are going to find a suitable lot on which to build. We can do that next year, after the baby is born. They will have all fall and winter to look around and think maybe might even get a better deal in the winter when the real estate business is slow here. I haven't mentioned it yet but that same snow can also sometimes cover up some unpleasant problems. They won't make any commitments without my OK, I'm sure.

The great day has arrived; we are all moved in! I have more stuff than this house can use, however the garage is as big as a barn and the excess is stored there for the time being. I told Grethel and Elaine that now that I did not have to pay all that rent on the van I could probably treat them to a little snack for dinner if they would like. Grethel murmured to Elaine, "See, I told you Ellie, he is not really as bad as people make him out to be. Elaine murmured in response, "You are absolutely right, Greth. I can't for the life of me understand why people must think so poorly of him." All this murmuring of course loud enough to be sure I could hear them.

I told them I would see about a reservation and went to use the telephone; fortunately, it had just that day been connected. When I returned, I told them I had just been informed that MacDonald's did not take reservations but they were not overly busy right then anyway. Furthermore, semi-casual dress would be acceptable before seven PM. I said I was happy we didn't have to get all dressed up just to get us a little snack. We just had time to clean up and beat the seven PM deadline I told them as I headed for the three-quarter bath to wash up. I didn't hear a sound as they went to use the other bath to repair their makeup and fix whatever else needed fixing.

I was wearing a sport coat and a shirt and tie as I waited for the ladies to make their appearance. As usual, they were a couple of knockouts. I swear they could probably look good wearing burlap bags and work boots. I said as soon as I saw them that they each looked like about ten million bucks each. Smart move on my part; I got a kiss from each of them. "OK", I said, "Let us get going if we want to beat that seven PM deadline. I've got the car out front." Off we went then, over to Main Street and out south. When we got to the road that headed up to the country club, I turned and started up toward the clubhouse. "I think you got turned around dear," Grethel told me. "This is not the way to MacDonald's and we can't get a meal here unless we are with a member." "Oh shucks," I said, "I guess I plumb forgot; old age creeping up on me I guess. I see there are only a few cars however; maybe they might just be glad to have some paying customers. Let's give it a try."

As we walked in, the club Manager was there in the foyer. He had a big smile for us as he said, "Welcome, Mr. Mayor and you, Mrs. Mayor; it is so nice to have you as members and Miss Mora, as usual it is always a pleasure to have you visit us. He ushered us to a nice booth near the windows and saw us seated with a lady on each side of me. Someone would be by shortly if we wished to order something from the bar he told us, as he handed out our menus. Grethel and Elaine had not said a word all this time.

They both turned on me when we were alone and vowed they were going to get even with me----later. I could depend on that. I chuckled then and told them, "While you gals were running all over this part of the state I thought I might as well do something useful and was able to get us a membership. After all, we *are* going to need somewhere to play golf, aren't we? Moreover, while the food might not be quite up to Elaine's standards it is not too bad. I hope you both approve. I did this especially for you my dear Grethel." She still had some of those kisses left and I got one right then. Elaine avowed then that, "Maybe I was not nearly as bad a person as everyone had been saying." We then had a very enjoyable dinner and pleasant conversation. It did appear I had done the right thing.

Chapter Four

WE WERE SITTING AT breakfast on a Sunday about two weeks later. I had begun a habit of making Sunday breakfast for us when we were at home. We had finished eating and were sipping our coffee as I glanced at the Sunday newspaper. I noticed then that Grethel was staring off into space again with that pensive look on her face. I figured this was as good a time as any so I said, "My dear Grethel, I have noticed that from time to time you seem to be staring off into space with a rather pensive look on your face. Tell me, is it your father that you are thinking about?" "Yes, my dear William," she told me; "for a long time when we had so many problems to handle and you were so sick I didn't have time to think about anything but you. Now that you are well and it looks like I have got you for sure I can't help wonder how he is and what has happened to him."

I told her I had suspected this for some time and I could certainly understand how she must feel. I knew how I would feel under the same circumstances. When I asked if she knew of any way that we might get in touch with him or anyone who would know about him, she shook her head sadly and said that unfortunately she did not.

I asked her about the Swiss bank accounts she had told me about and the possibility her father may have contacted those banks. Perhaps we should contact them. If money had been withdrawn from those accounts, it would indicate that her father might have escaped from the hands of the East German state police. Of course, someone else could possibly have gotten the numbers from him and accessed the accounts. I said then, we knew Elaine was expecting Al in town soon; why didn't we wait and see what ideas he may have that might help us?

"William, you are such a thoughtful husband," Grethel said, "and if my father is alive I would dearly love to have him know that I *do* have such a wonderful husband and will have a grandchild for him to see before very long." I told her, OK, that is what we would do. We cannot just go on like this forever never knowing what has happened to him. I said, "You know my dear, I would do anything I could to insure your happiness." Aah, another of those special kisses; getting used to them surely has been easy.

CHAPTER FIVE

WE TOOK ELAINE AND AL to dinner at the Country Club the next Saturday. It was the first time we had taken guests other than the time I surprised Grethel and Elaine. We had been here with Vern and Francine but they are members here also. Vern had joined several years ago, shortly after his promotion to Senior Deputy. We had agreed to meet our guests at the club and Grethel and I were there ahead of time waiting for them in the lobby. They were there right on the dot, both with great big smiles; the cat that ate the canary kind. They must be up to something.

The head waitress/hostess led to us to our table, by a window as I had asked for. It was still light enough that we could enjoy the view out over the course for a while. It soon became obvious why the big smiles we had been seeing. Elaine was careful to reach out for her water glass with her *left* hand and to hold it out there just long enough. Grethel let out a gasp. "William," she whispered. "Look at Elaine's hand? "Just a second my dear," I said. "Let me get my sunglasses out and I surely will."

Then, I took Elaine's hand in mine and examined it at some length, turning her palm over several times as I peered closely at her ring. Finally I said, "You know Elaine, my dear, I do think this may be the prettiest friendship ring I have seen for some time. "Stop teasing her, William," Grethel chimed in. "You *know* that is an engagement ring." I took Elaine's hand again, peered closely at the ring and then said, "By George, Grethel, I do believe you may be right, my dear. Where in the world did you *find it*, Elaine?" Elaine gave me a punch on the arm then sputtering, "you nitwit; you know darn well I didn't *find* it." "Goodness gracious, my dear Elaine," I gasped; "Don't tell me you went out and *bought* this gorgeous example of the jeweler's art?" Elaine was sputtering by now, trying to think of words but before she could I continued,

"Oh no, Elaine, please, please, don't tell me; surely it cannot be *stolen*. Remember, I am duty bound, as an honorary deputy of this county, to see that the law is upheld." Al who had been sitting there chuckling, then burst out laughing. "You know, I swear this is the funniest thing I have heard since Abbot and Costello and '*Who's on first*," he said. I think I can get you two some bookings into some of the better lounge shows. We all had a good laugh then and Grethel and I gave our good friends out best wishes for their future happiness. We also told them what a beautiful engagement ring it truly was.

If you think that was funny, you should have heard Al and me trying to explain about Abbot and Costello and their famous routine to Grethel who had not only, never had heard of them but knew even less about the game of baseball. We gave up on that rather soon and I ordered a bottle of champagne so we could properly toast our friend's engagement. Grethel had only a small sip as I made the toast to our friend's future happiness, remarking to Elaine that she did not wish to jeopardize the health of any of Dear William's future numerous offspring. Elaine allowed that of course, in that respect, one could never be too careful.

Elaine said then that she must apologize. She had forgotten to bring the book she had purchased for us. It had lists of literally thousands of names for babies. She knew if there were the *numerous* offspring that, *Dear William*, had promised Grethel, finding enough names might prove to be an onerous chore. Grethel certainly did not want to be *forced* to perhaps numbering them or perhaps worse, resort to alphabetizing them. "Can't you just see it, Greth," she continued;"maybe odd numbers for boys and even for the girls. I can just hear you calling them to come home for dinner: *Oh One and three, find two, four, five and six and come in for dinner now please.* When he could stop laughing, Al said, "All right already, enough is enough, let me know when you guys are ready and I'll get you your lounge show bookings in Vegas or Reno if you prefer. As your agent, I will soon be rich!

Well we did settle down and had a very nice dinner. Over coffee, Grethel told Al about her father. She had told Elaine all about it some time ago. I also gave my thoughts on a way I had thought we might get information about him through the Swiss banks. Al said how sorry he was to hear what had happened to Grethel's father and realized how this uncertainty had to be a constant, nagging source of worry. He did however have some reservations about my suggestion.

Of course, of course; I don't know why that did not occur to me before now. Another, *Senior Moment*, I suppose. Obviously, if we sent the numbers to someone to check the accounts there was nothing to prevent that person from withdrawing any money that might be there, if the accounts still existed, and then telling us, that when checking, it was found the accounts had been closed and there was no further information available.

If these accounts *were* intact, from the information Grethel had gotten on her last visit to Zurich, there should be some substantial amounts on deposit. This then posed a problem. Grethel said she would *never* go back to Europe. After her last experience there, she was still terrified that something might happen to her if she returned and also she did not in any way want to jeopardize her baby, Well, I guess that feeling is understandable.

Al suggested then, "You know, Bill, you have obviously shown that you can handle yourself pretty well. You might be the logical one to undertake this preliminary investigation. It shouldn't take too long to fly over there and do what has to be done. If the accounts are still intact, you might want to see about having them transferred here or at least to different accounts in Switzerland. That might help safeguard having them fall into the wrong hands. If Grethel's Dad hasn't accessed the accounts by now it would appear he is not going to do so for whatever reasons. That thought of course brought tears to Grethel's eyes.

Al was all apologies. He had not meant to distress Grethel. I put my arms around her and told her not to be so upset. I pointed out then that Al was right. I was the logical one to undertake this job. Then she did begin to weep big tears and asked, "But what if something happens to *you* William? What would I ever do? Whenever you go off, something always happens to put you in danger. I want you to stay here with me." Elaine chimed in with, "Grethel is right, Bill; you need to be here where we can watch you. Whenever you go off alone you get into some kind of mischief. Do you think we could stand worrying about what you are up to all the time you are out of our sight? "Well for crying out loud; you would think I must be some little kid.

I said to them, "Listen, you two; I guess you both know that you are my favorite people in the whole world. I am more flattered than you can realize to know that you are both so concerned about my welfare. As Al has observed however, I have demonstrated that I can take care of myself pretty well. In any event, how difficult or dangerous can it be to pop over there and make a few inquiries? A couple days here and there; what danger can there be for goodness sake? It should just be a simple job. Grethel means more to me than anything and it is just ridiculous to expect me to sit on my hands and do nothing to ease her unhappiness and, ladies, the sooner I get started the sooner I will be home. After all," I said, "You all know I must be back home well before the first of my *humorous* children arrive." Of course, both ladies chimed in then, in unison, "numerous." I knew that would get them. We all chuckled then. I guess I had them convinced, even if they weren't particularly happy about what I planned to do. It was something however, that must be done. I guess they could see that and that there was no one else right now except me who could do it. Elaine agreed then that she would move in with Grethel while I was away.

Well, it was time to get cracking. I wanted to get there and back in as short a time as possible. I didn't want people to start worrying if I was gone for too long a time. Al was able to pull a few strings and get me a passport in a few days. It sometimes helps to have a friend in the Federal Bureau of Investigation doesn't it? I had no idea what Grethel's dad looked like and asked her if she might not have a picture of him somewhere. She had me get the big box in which she had dumped the contents of her suitcases we had taken from the car in Leevining where we had discovered Joachim's remains. She thought she might have one among the things she had brought from Wiesbaden.

Grethel had me go through the box with her. She said likely we could just put a lot of the stuff in the trash. She found several photos of her father but except for one that was three years old, the others were all too old to be of use to me. I made copies of the best one on my scanner/ copier and returned the original to Grethel.

As we were separating things in piles and putting the discards in a trash bag, I picked up a little crumpled up ball of paper and asked Grethel, "What in the world prompted you to save something like this?" "Oh, I had forgotten all about that," she said. "Do you remember when you asked me to search through the things in my suitcase for anything that Emil or Joachim might have put in them besides the guns? That was the only thing I saw. Why would they ever put something like that in with my things? I had forgotten all about it. You may remember we had a lot of things on our minds at the time." I sure did remember. I also remember now asking her to check. I too had forgotten all about it. I smoothed out the note-sized paper. I guess we should check it before tossing it out.

Well, that was strange. There were the letters SB. Under that were two rows of numbers and under that, the letter Z; that was all. I showed the slip to Grethel and asked what she could make of it. After examining it a few minutes, she said that those numbers looked similar to ones she had for the accounts her father had opened in the Swiss banks. We knew, she reminded me, that Emil and Joachim had been in Switzerland at the time she was there. Grethel spoke German like a native, which is the language used in much of Switzerland, a place she had visited a number of times. SB, she thought could possibly stand for Schweizerisher Bankverin, one of the largest banking houses in Switzerland. Maybe the Z indicated their branch in Zürich, the chief banking city in the country. I decided it might be a good idea to hold onto the paper and take it with me to Switzerland next week. I wrote Grethel's suggested bank name on the back of the slip.

I asked Grethel if either her Aunt Ethel or Aunt Gretchen were still alive. If so maybe they may have had some contact with her father. Neither of them of course would have any idea of the whereabouts of Grethel or for that matter even if *she* were alive. As far as she knew, her father had not had any contact with either of them for some time. All she had, if she could find the information among her things, were the cities in which they lived when she had last heard of them. She would try to dig out that information for me before I left.

CHAPTER SIX

WELL I'M ON MY way. I will change planes in LaGuardia and fly to Heathrow. I'll first try to find Grethel's Aunt Ethel in the city of Twyford. That appears to be not too far from London, just a little west of Slough, halfway between Maidenhead and Reading, according to the map I checked. Assuming that is the right Twyford. It appears there may be more than one city of that name.

I finally made it into the city of London. What a long and boring trip! It seems like I have been on the way here for a week and not just almost two days. I was so tired all I wanted to do was find a place to sleep. At the prices for lodging I'm seeing I better sleep like a log and even then I don't think I will be getting my money's worth. Living is sure a lot easier----and cheaper where I come from.

I slept until ten the next morning and I was still tired. I decided to delay another day and rest up a bit. I may be getting a tad too old for this sort of thing. I was going to order room service for some breakfast until I saw the prices. I decided then to get up and see if I might find a place to eat not quite so expensive. When I asked the Concierge to recommend a nearby pub where I might get something to eat, he recommended the Roaring Bull only a block distant and to that establishment I made my way.

Well by then, it was just about lunchtime so I asked if they could fix me something to go with the glass of Guinness I had ordered. I told the barkeep I was a stranger in the city and would rely on his good judgment. English brews take a little getting used to I guess but the Guinness wasn't too bad and I must admit they did set out a nice lunch for me. I surely wasn't hungry when I finally paid up and left.

I decided I wasn't going to do much today so I now decided to splurge and hire one of the famous London Taxis. I told the cabbie I hired that I was newly arrived in the city and asked could he show me the sights he thought a stranger to his city should see? He surely did know his city and I guess I saw everything in the heart of the city I should see. At the prices charged by London cabbies, I guess you have a right to expect them to be very knowledgeable. The one I had sure knew his stuff. When he learned I was going to rent a car and drive to Twyford, he drove me on the route from my hotel that would get me off in the right direction. Maybe that will save me some grief. We shall soon find out. It is going to be scary enough driving on the wrong side of the road. The traffic is just terrible; even worse than downtown L.A. during the rush hours, which now seems to be just about all day long.

The next morning I figured I was probably as rested as I would ever be and I might just as well get on my way. I had arranged for a rental car the night before and, as I had asked, it was awaiting my pleasure in front of the hotel. My luggage was loaded in "the boot". It is a good thing I had gotten all those pointers from the cabbie yesterday; it took me a whole mile or was it a kilometer, before I had become hopelessly lost.

After driving around in what likely were circles I had to give up. I had managed to get myself by then into a really crummy looking part of the city. It appeared I had come to a stop in front of some kind of pubic house. I got out my map to see if I could find where I was. It might as well have been in Chinese, as I could not make head or tail of what I was looking at. It was only nine-thirty in the morning but the pub was already open. Perhaps they never closed. I wonder who goes to a pub at this hour. Nothing else was open nearby that I could see so I thought I would see if these people, whoever they were, might be able to help me out with some directions.

As soon as I got inside the place, it became immediately apparent that coming in here might not have been the smartest move I could have made. In addition to being dirty, dingy and smelly, I could see I was the only one with a white face on the premises and none of those looking back at me were the least bit friendly. All talking had ceased when I had stepped inside.

Well, what the hell; with map in hand I approached the bar and explained my need for assistance in getting some directions. The surly individual behind the bar informed me; "this was not some public service agency that dispensed free information." I asked how much it might cost for someone to show me on my map just where I was and the barkeep sneered that likely a quid would do it. I wasn't sure exactly what a quid was but put some money on the bar and the barman and several others took a look at my map. Finally the barman put a finger with about six week's accumulation of some noxious substances under the nail on my map and said, "that's where you are sport, now you and yer bleedin' map can take yerself off. We don't need the likes o your kind in 'ere."

By now, I just wanted to get out of this place anyway. As I made my way to the door, I noticed another of the patrons also preparing to leave. As I got outside, there, standing by my car, was yet another young tough. A delightful specimen of London youth; dirt, grime, tattoos, nose rings, leather jacket, the works. It looks now like maybe I had been set up. Who would ever expect this could happen in a city like London and in broad daylight. I guess I was really in the wrong part of town. Of course, there was not a Policeman in sight; in fact, I didn't see anyone else to whom I might turn to for help. Maybe I had a bit of a "*sticky wicket*" right now, as I think they say over here.

I decided to just try and get into the car and take off but, as I reached to unlock the door, the young tough pushed me away from the door and informed me there was a tax on foreigners driving through this neighborhood; hand over my watch and wallet. I asked what would happen if I didn't and at that moment a switchblade appeared in his hand. I was informed then to hand over my watch and wallet *now* or I would soon be "*wearing my guts for garters*". Must be some kind of colloquial expression they use in this neighborhood.

There I was, with nothing to defend myself. I was afraid that even if I were to hand over my wallet and watch I still might be killed or at best maybe stabbed. That's when I heard, "Drop the knife mister scum bag or you are going to have a nice big smile right under your chin," The person I had seen following me out was not one of the assailants as I had supposed. He had grabbed, "Mister Scum Bag", by his greasy ponytail and now held a long curved knife against his throat. Scum Bag promptly dropped *his* knife, which I promptly kicked into the gutter. My helper suggested I use my car phone to phone the Bobbies. Maybe then, we might give Scum Bag a running start before they arrived. With our description, they should pick him up in short order anyway. Likely, he could figure on at least twenty years in the slammer with the record he no doubt had. When he said, "Scram" and let go his ponytail, Scum

Bag took off as if he had a rocket up his butt. I didn't have a car phone but of course he didn't know that.

Now I had a chance to look at my benefactor. He was a little taller than I, had a small mustache and beard and was wearing a turban. I figured from his appearance that likely he must be from India. I told him I was very much in his debt but he said he was most happy I had arrived when I did. He also had gotten to this place purely by chance and had been trying to think of a way to exit the place when I came in. I told him, "From your appearance, sir, I would guess you are a Sikh." "But no, not at all, my friend," he assured me. "It is true I have not been sleeping well lately and perhaps may appear to you, Sir, to be just a trifle peckish but assuredly notta seek; actually I am in quite good health." Then he started laughing, adding, "Thank you kind sir for that opening; you don't know how long I have been waiting to use that routine."

"Actually, my name is Singh," he informed me; "a rather common name among us Sikhs as you may know. You may not believe it but I have come here to get into the entertainment business. I have worked a little in India's Bollywood and I sing, dance and do some acting. I have been billing myself as Singh, the singing Sikh. A rather catchy title don't you think?" I told him that after hearing him I thought likely he should work up a comedy routine. At any rate, I was most grateful for his timely help, introduced myself and asked if there was any way I could possibly be of assistance to him.

He said he would appreciate a ride out of this neighborhood. He too had wound up here by accident as he was out exploring the city. Fortunately, he had fit into the color scheme around here somewhat better than I did but he was most uncomfortable in this kind of an environment. I told him to hop into the car with me and when he did so handed him the map and told him where I was going. He said if I didn't mind he would ride with me as far as Slough. He had a cousin living there who had offered to put him up for a few days. He would direct me. As I probably knew, Slough was on my way to the city of Twyford. I told him I would welcome his company and driving directions.

I did make it out of town and in the right direction thanks to the help of my friend, The Singing Sikh. Of course, I also added a fistful of gray hairs and took about five years off my life but I made it. I'm not sure how I did it but after letting my friend off in Slough, I found myself in the town of Twyford not too long thereafter. I sure hope Grethel never finds about this little escapade; she would kill me for sure.

Aunt Ethel's last name is Thatcher. There must be a couple million Thatchers here in England, however. No doubt, that was a surname dating back to ancient times and was descriptive of a person who thatched roofs for his livelihood; such as John the Thatcher. I guess there are still people that do thatching, as there are still a few cottages about that still have thatched roofs. Likely, however most of those doing that kind of work now are not named Thatcher. Do you suppose some may be called, "Roofer", Jack the Roofer maybe? Nah, not likely, but anyway, back to business.

After making a few enquiries (They *enquire* over here.) I located the post office. I figured that might be a good place to start and it was. When I explained who I was and that I was married to Mrs. Thatcher's niece they told me that yes, the Major and Mrs. Thatcher had lived here in Twyford since before the War. They were highly respected in this city. After explaining that I was new to the country, they gave me explicit directions to the Thatcher "cottage".

Well, after stopping several times for additional directions, I found it. For a *cottage*, it looked to be pretty good sized. It looked to be quite old and was most attractive with beautiful flowers in profusion in the gardens. A tall gray-haired man, with a trim military mustache, answered the door when I rang. I swear, he could have been picked by Central Casting to play the part of a retired British Army officer. He assured me I had found the correct address when I asked and then observed, "American are you not?" I said he was correct and gave my name and said that I was married to Mrs. Thatcher's niece, Grethel Evans. It was on her behalf that I had come to see them. She had lost track of her father and she was hoping his sister might have some recent word from him.

"Well do come in my dear boy," he said, stepping aside and opening the door for me. He sat me down and said, "My dear Ethel will return from her shopping shortly. I know she will want to talk to you. She has wondered so often about what has happened to her niece." Just then, we heard a car pulling up in their driveway and Major Thatcher said that must be his wife now. If I would just relax for a moment, he would intercept her and help bring in the groceries and advise her I was here. He was back almost at once and said that his wife was so excited that

I had come. She must go back to the market at once. She knew I must be starving and she must prepare a suitable luncheon for us as soon as she returned. The Major chuckled and said they hadn't had so much excitement around here for a long time; he was so glad I was there.

While we were waiting, he asked me what I did and wondered if I had been in military service during the war. I told him that right now, I was mostly retired but yes, I had been in the service and actually had been in on the Normandy invasion, landing on Utah Beach. Fortunately not right on D Day I told him or I would likely not be here today. I finally wound up with four battle stars on my ETO ribbon by war's end I said. Lieutenant was the highest rank I made before being discharged to inactive service. I had left military service when the war ended. . He came over then, shook my hand, and declared we were comrades in arms. He had landed on Sword Beach, also fortunately not on D Day. Then like all vets when they are getting acquainted, we began sharing wartime experiences and were so engaged when Mrs. Thatcher came bustling in with her arms full of packages. She gave me a big hug and said she was so pleased I had come to them. She was looking forward to hearing all about her niece. Turning to the Major, she said that this was such a special occasion, why did he not fix a couple drinks for the two of us while she got some food together for us.

The Major thought that was just a "Capital" idea and proceeded to fix a glass of Scotch for each of us. He said, "You know, my boy, I used to drink this stuff neat, the British way. I have found however that now I am a little older the American way with ice and a little water seems to be better for me. Is that alright with you?" I said I couldn't think of anything better and he proceeded to fix us up. The Scotch was a brand with which I was not familiar but was very good I discovered and I complemented the Major on his selection.

The Major had retired after thirty-five years of service in the army. He had a part ownership in a small bookstore now and worked there occasionally. I said I had been a civil servant after the war and then ran my own business for a while but now I was mostly retired and was kept pretty busy by Grethel whenever I had a spare moment. Before we married I had spent some time painting landscapes and then doing some writing. I also dabbled a little with music when I was not otherwise occupied. My late wife I told him had passed away some years ago. I promised to tell them both how I had met and married Grethel over lunch.

Mrs. Thatcher soon had put out a beautiful lunch for us and had set a festive table with flowers from her garden for decoration. While we ate, I told the story about how Grethel and I had met and then married. You have all heard that before so I won't go over it again. I guess they must have found it all pretty interesting, at any rate they did not utter a word until I had finished. Of course, I didn't include all the details. If I had, it would have taken forever. I did want them to know that we were very concerned about Grethel's father and covered what we knew about his last days in some detail.

Ethel Thatcher said, when I had finished, "William, I do hope you do not mind if I call you by your first name but I am sure you have left out many important details and likely will have to wait to hear them when I can telephone to Grethel. I can sense however that probably you saved her life, did you not?" I said I figured I just happened to be in the right place at the right time, anyone else would have done the same under those particular circumstances. The Major harrumphed then and said, "Nonsense, Leftenant, I can tell from what you have obviously left out of your story that most likely you deserve a hero's welcome from us. I am so proud that you have come to our house. We will of course do whatever we can to help you in your endeavors.

When they learned I had driven out from London they insisted I spend the night with them in their guest room. I thanked them and said it would please me to have the opportunity to get to know them better. I also suggested that if there was a nice restaurant they could recommend I would like to take them to dinner. It was agreed, that is what we would do. I moved my suitcase into the room they showed me and Ethel said she had a hunch that by now I would like a good wash-up and a little nap before the Major and I had drinks before we went out to eat. I said that really sounded like a lovely idea. The Major said how about fiveish for cocktails and in the meantime he would phone in dinner reservations for us. I slept like a log! Up to now, it had been one busy day!

I felt much rested by the time I had put on some more presentable clothes and joined the Major and Ethel for cocktails. I had some pictures of the wedding and brought them out for their inspection. They were enchanted with the pictures of Grethel and said she was even more beautiful than they had remembered. I told Ethel I thought the family resemblance was obvious which of course pleased her. I suggested she select one of the photos to keep which she did.

We had time for one more small drink and then we were off to dinner. The major drove, thank goodness! It was only a half hour drive but even so, I had no idea where we were. Thankfully, I was not the one who had to find the route back to the cottage. They told me that the Red Lion Inn where we were dining was over three hundred years old. It was very interesting and we had an excellent dinner with a good wine. I complemented the Major on his excellent choice of restaurants.

In our conversation over dinner, they both agreed that it had been a number of years since they had any word from Evan Evans. Now that they had heard my story, they too were worried about what may have happened to him. The last they had heard of him he was still in the Foreign Service. They did have an address for Gretchen Groenwald fortunately and that will be of help. Calling on her is to be next on my agenda.

Over breakfast the next morning I invited them to visit us in California after the baby was born. I promised they would have an enjoyable time. They said they would plan on that; it had been a long time since they had been on a real holiday. Using the map the Major gave me I headed for Heathrow right after breakfast. I had given Ethel our telephone number in California and she had said she would be phoning later when the rates were better. I had assured her that Grethel would be happy to hear I had arrived safe and sound. I hadn't mentioned the trouble I had had even getting out of London. I really had been pretty dumb. Maybe I will save that little story about the Singing Sikh for a later time.

I was able to book a direct flight to Templehof. We were there in a relatively short time. It seems strange to me that the big cities of Europe are so close together. It also seems strange that they have here all these relatively small countries that all have different customs and speak different languages. I guess it all stems from centuries ago when people just did not travel far from their home as the general means of travel then was by walking.

I found that Gretchen Groenwald's address was in East Berlin, or what had been East Berlin until about a year ago when the Berlin Wall came down. Now there was just one Berlin and one Germany. I'm sure if the Communists were still running things I would have had a difficult if not impossible time in ever finding her. It might have been forbidden then and likely most dangerous to even try. I got a rental car at the airport using my American Express credit card and started out. The car rental people had supplied me with a map and circled the place I wanted to find. The traffic turned out to be as bad as London but at least here, they drive on the proper side of the road. I noticed that traffic thinned considerably when I got into the East section.

It seemed almost everyone around the airport spoke or understood English. I found when I had gotten into the East zone that was not the case. I found out soon that many street signs were still missing and I was getting pretty confused. When I would stop and try to ask directions, All I got were blank looks and a shake of the head. I finally spotted someone who looked like he might be a police officer of some kind and approached him with my map. Pointing to the circled place on the map I tried, "Kennen zie wo ist, Bitte." "Ah," he answered; "You are perhaps lost?" I guess I must have found the only person in East Berlin who spoke English.

After a brief chat, during which he welcomed me to the eastern part of the city, he showed me on my map where I was. Then he suggested that I count each of the streets as I proceeded rather than try to read names, which, even if they were present, I likely could not understand. That made sense and proceeding in that manner before long I thought I must be at the address that I sought.

What a depressing looking building! It was one of six identical buildings. These were in an apartment complex the Communists had built right after the war, first bulldozing a tract of bombed-out and ruined buildings. I have lived in army barracks that were much cheerier in aspect than this. There wasn't a blade of grass, tree or a shrub of any kind to be seen. It looked just like a prison without a fence around it. I guess that is more or less, what it was until just recently. I entered the grim building entrance and noted there was no one in the building-watcher's cubicle. Now, how do I find Grethel's Aunt Gretchen? There was no building directory and I couldn't see any clue on how you were supposed to locate anyone in the building.

I was standing there, literally scratching my head, when a youngish sort of man entered the building. He looked like he might live here so I approached him and tried my limited German saying, "Bitte, mien

Herr, Kennen zie wo ist Frau Groenwald?" Then I held my breath. He likely could not understand a word of my fractured German.

"Ah, Frau Groenwald," he said with a big smile and then proceeded to rattle on in German occasionally pointing upward. Finally, I held up my hand, stop and tried, "Bitte, mien Herr, Ich nicht verstehn Deutch. Maybe you speak a little English?" "But of course," he answered, "but only a little amount." I told him then whenever I had asked anyone if they spoke English they ignored me. He told me that old habits are hard to break. The East German State Police, the Stasi as they were called, rightfully discouraged people from speaking with foreigners. To do so, until recently, might get you detention time or sometimes even something worse.

It turned out that I could find the *fraulein* on the fourth floor, the apartment at the end of the hall on the left. Should I need a guide or help while here in East Berlin please call upon him. He would be happy to be of service. He was Bruno. I would find him on the second floor. His name was on the door, "Hauptmann". I thanked him and started up the stairs. I guess the decadence of elevators has not yet reached this far east.

Well anyway, the hall was clean and quiet. I proceeded as directed and found a "G" was painted on the door at the end of the hall. This must be the place. I knocked on the door a couple times and called out "Frau Groenwald, Bitte". I couldn't think of any other German words that might be of use. Maybe I'm not too well prepared for this expedition. I tried again with "Frau Groenwald, Bitte" without any results.

Finally, I opted to try English and announced, "I am your niece Grethel Evans husband. She has sent me to find information about her father who is missing." German had not been working. If English didn't either I am going to have a problem. Perhaps there is no one home. Then what do I do? At last, aha, the door opened a crack. I could see though it was still fastened with a number of chains to keep it from opening farther. A blue eye was behind the crack observing me. A voice asked, "Are you American?" I said that I was and when asked, that Grethel's father was named Evan Evans.

The door shut followed by the sound of clanking chains and other sounds that sounded vaguely like the opening of a bank vault. The door opened then, and there stood a slightly younger version of my Grethel.

You could have knocked me over with a feather. The resemblance was uncanny. I stood there with my mouth hanging open, speechless. Finally I said, "You must excuse my staring, miss but you look almost exactly like my wife, Grethel." She laughed then, held out her hand and said, I guess I am Grethel's cousin. I'm Elke. I complemented her on how well she spoke English and she said she had studied it in school. She had kept up with further study of the language at her father's insistence. She and her close friends practiced speaking it frequently with each other, partly because they knew the Communist authorities did not like it; then muttering under her breath, "the lousy bastards".

I explained then why I had come here to see Grethel's Aunt Gretchen. Elke explained that her mother was out trying to find a shop that might have some groceries. They were just about out of everything. When I asked why they did not go into the western part of the city where it appeared the stores were all very well stocked she said they had no car and besides the goods there were too expensive for them and their money would not go very far. At any rate, her mother should be home soon and as long as I was here, she would not bother fastening up all the locks again. I asked her then if this was such a dangerous place to live and she said that yes, it was for two women living alone. I guess it must be just great having to live in a place that was not only depressing as hell but was also dangerous as well. That's when we heard approaching footsteps and then a soft knocking that was obviously some kind of code. Elke announced, "There is mother now."

A tired looking lady came in. She had started to scold Elke for not having the chains on the door until she noticed me standing there. Elke introduced me as Grethel's husband and explained why I was there. At least I assume that is what she was doing as all this was carried out in rapid German. Aunt Gretchen then turned to me, held out her hand and said, "Welkommen". I replied "Danke," and then explained to Elke that I had just about exhausted my limited fund of German words and she explained this to her mother.

Elke said that her mother had had little success in her shopping and was now worried about how she was going to provide a meal for their guest. I asked Elke if there was not some place that I could take them both for dinner. I had a rental car, which I had parked down in front of the building. Perhaps I could also take them shopping somewhere where they might have a better selection than Aunt Gretchen had found available around here. When Elke said that their finances would not permit such luxuries, I protested. After all, we were the same family and I felt it my privilege to do this for them. When Elke explained all this to her mother, she nodded shyly, accepting my offer. I could see she was making every effort that I not to see her tears. Well, we certainly cannot allow this condition to continue. I noticed there was no evidence of Herr Groenwald but decided not to make mention of that at this time.

As it was too early to go out for dinner, I suggested maybe it would be a good time for us to go grocery shopping. The ladies discussed this and then Elke said that if I did not mind, her mother would stay home and rest up a little after her tiring day. She wanted to be able to enjoy our dinner. Elke would go with me and provide directions. She said that maybe we could go back to the West zone where there was a better selection and I agreed that sounded like a good idea.

We finally located a market that looked much like our supermarkets at home. Elke was amazed at the variety and number of things available. Without a car, they had not yet been able to see the stores in the western part of the city. She said, "Oh, William, you have no idea what it was like living in the East Zone. We seemed never to be able to find the things we needed. Most of the things available were things we neither wanted nor could use." Well, I made sure we had a goodly supply of things before we headed back. Their refrigerator was so tiny I could not get as much meat as I thought they should have. Elke assured me that too much of what I wanted to buy would spoil before they could use it.

When we got back to the apartment, I noticed that apparently Aunt Gretchen had gotten her nap; she looked much more rested now. She had also changed her clothes and I suspect that it was her best dress that she was now wearing. She was also wearing some makeup now and looked like an entirely different person from the tired, little old lady I had seen just a little while ago.

She was overjoyed with the supplies we had brought home. There was enough now that she could fix a meal for us right here. I said that no, I was looking forward to taking them to dinner. It would give us all a chance to be better acquainted. It was already time for us to go then and I suggested we do so. I also told them I was relying on them to pick out a really good restaurant where they knew we could get a nice meal. It was well I had Elke as a guide. I'm sure on my own I would have been hopelessly lost.

We did find a nice restaurant and the ladies had a wonderful time. Grethel's aunt had not been to such a place since before the Communists had taken over. Elke never had and believed she could get used to this sort of thing without hardly any trouble at all. They were having such a pleasant meal that they did not want to spoil our good time by discussing their situation now. We would talk when we got back to the apartment. They insisted I must stay with them. I would use Elke's room and she would share her mother's. They would show me later where I could store my car where it would be safe.

We had been having such a good time eating and talking that it was late when we finally left the restaurant. The safe car storage was in a small warehouse a block from the apartment complex. For a small fee, they agreed to store my rental car. What a gloomy and eerie place this neighborhood was after dark. I didn't see any other people about. The ladies said they were glad I was with them. Elke said they almost never ventured out at night.

We finally got back to the apartment and settled in to talk. Elke of course was out interpreter. I explained what we knew of Grethel's father and that I had come here to try to find out if he was still alive. They said that those same Stasi had also arrested Herr Groenwald. He had been too vocal too long in is criticism of the Communists. It was just a little more than two years ago, that he had been taken off to prison. He was declared to be, "an enemy of the state". Six months passed by with no word from him. They received word then that he had been involved in an accident in the prison laundry and had died.

Gustav Groenwald had been a schoolteacher. When they no longer had his income, they soon had to give up their small home. They were forced by the Communist government to live now in these wretched surroundings to which they had been assigned. They were very bitter. They, and especially Elke, were having a difficult time. Because she was attractive, she had been under constant pressure to marry or to live with some party functionary or other in order that "their life would be more pleasant". She had also found that only if she agreed to sleep with some bureaucrat or other could she expect to get any good job paying enough for them to live on. Their circumstances were becoming desperate and it appeared she soon must agree and do as she was being asked, if they were to keep from starving. They had been hoping that now that the wall was down, the country was now again united and they were no longer prisoners, they could find some escape from this situation before it was too late.

They were sorry to hear about the misfortunes of Grethel's father and that he also had run afoul of the dreaded Stasi. They had been hated here almost universally by all those not a part of their network of informers and spies. The Stasi had had secret informer all over the country, just like the Nazis before them. It had been estimated that there may have been at least one hundred thousand of them. It was only now that they were beginning to be uncovered. Bruno, they had learned, was the Stasi informer in their building. They also had recently found out, Bruno was the person who had arranged for their assignment to this particular building. Bruno still had his "connections" they believed and he also was one of those that had been pressuring Elke for her favors. If it looked like she must go that route, she had decided probably it must be with Bruno, as he seemed least objectionable of those she had seen.

They were sorry but they had heard nothing of or from Evan Evans. That was not surprising however. He would have had a difficult time in finding them or in contacting them if he had while the Communists controlled everything.

I told them both then they were not to worry about Elke having to do anything she did not want to do. I had just decided that I should no doubt hire her. That only made good sense. I would need an interpreter if I was to conduct my investigations and it was logical that I should hire my wife's cousin who was obviously well qualified for the job. They both sighed with relief when Elke relayed this information to her mother. Now, over the next few days, I told them, we must decide what Elke's mother was to do while we were conducting our investigations.

After breakfast the next morning I suggested we should all go clothes shopping that day. Elke would need some things if she were going to be travelling with me. I vowed to myself that we would see that Gretchen had a new dress or two as well. They were both so excited at this prospect. It did my heart good to see them so happy.

Well, obviously I had never in Berlin before and Elke said she and her mother did not know much more about the stores in west part of the city than I did. We did quite a little bit of driving around therefore before we had found the shops we needed. Have you ever been shopping with ladies? It has got to be the most exhausting thing a man can do! Believe me! Both ladies told me that they were concerned that I would be spending too much money. I told them the rate of exchange was not too bad and I knew Grethel would be very upset with me if I did not see that they were both properly outfitted for their travels.

It had taken us quite some time to find the right stores and by the time we had finished shopping, we had spent the whole day. I was pooped! I told the ladies that now, I was worn out. I suggested we must find a place where we could get a libation of some kind and then a meal of some sort also. I really needed to rebuild my strength. I said we would then go home and I expected to sleep for three days, maybe more. The ladies thought that was hilarious; they were both as fresh as daisies.

The place we settled on served a glass of quite good beer and with that we had a delicious dinner of sauerbraten, served with sweet and sour red cabbage and potato pancakes. When we finished dinner, I told the ladies I thought likely now I would probably survive until the morrow. They thought I was being so droll. With Elke's guidance, we finally found the little warehouse again and left the car. I vaguely recall the walk (staggering) to the apartment and negotiating the forty flights of stairs and falling into bed. I thought I had died but it turned out that I was only unconscious.

It appeared that I must have wound up in Valhalla or somewhere very similar. As consciousness returned, I was aware of the glorious aroma of freshly brewing coffee and other good things I could not yet identify. Then I spotted Gretchen in the doorway. When she saw my eyes were open she said, "Gooten morgen, Wilhelm; schlaffen zie wohl"? When I answered, "Gooten morgen, Gretchen" she said, Wilst du Kaffee haben, Wilhelm? I gasped that that just might save my life. She figured I must have uttered some kind of affirmative response and came in and put a steaming cup of coffee on the nightstand next to the bed saying," essen fimfzehn minuten, Wilhelm". I guessed that must mean I had better get up and dressed and that is what I did. I realized then that I was so hungry I swear I could have eaten a horse.

What a fantastic breakfast Gretchen had fixed for me! I told her I thought she should open her own restaurant and she would soon be rich. She laughed when Elke translate for her. It was amazing but it seemed I had completely recovered from yesterday's ordeal. Perhaps the thimble full of Schnapps Gretchen had given me with my coffee had helped speed my recovery. Well anyway, likely it didn't hurt.

I explained over breakfast that now I must go to Switzerland to continue my investigation. I had hoped they or the Thatchers, who I had just been visiting, would have information I could use but unfortunately, that was not to be. Elke would do the interpreting for me as necessary. I wanted to talk to the Major before I left Berlin and will do that from the airport. I must arrange our transportation, which I will do while I am there. I left the ladies at the apartment. I felt sure I could now find my way back to the airport and I did so, eventually.

I spoke with both Ethel and the Major and they were both appalled when I explained the situation in which I had found the ladies. I told them that Elke would accompany me and do any interpreting for me that was necessary but I was concerned about leaving Gretchen alone while we were travelling. I also explained that Gretchen spoke almost no English. The Major insisted I send her along to them. I told him I thought that likely was the best solution. When I told him I would be sending along some funds to help pay for her upkeep he would have none of that. Family was family, he said; they would manage just fine. He reminded me then the ladies would both need passports if they were to leave the country. Of course, of course, why hadn't I thought of that? Another of those "senior moments" I guess. Obviously, I couldn't make transportation arrangements either until the matter of passports was taken care of. Well, back to the compound.

I swear all they needed was a few armed guards standing around the buildings and you would be certain you were visiting a prison complex. Of course, the ladies did not have passports. No one in the East Zone had one after the Communist government discovered all the best and brightest of the country were leaving for greener pastures. The new freedoms, with the change of government, were going to take some getting used to. I imagine the men in the Kremlin must be having kittens. How unfortunate.

At dinnertime, I brought up the problem of obtaining passports. Neither of the ladies had any idea how one went about getting one. No one that they knew had ever gotten one. Most likely, there must be some office in Berlin or perhaps Bonn that handled such matters, they suggested. We must determine just where to go I guess. I asked them if maybe Bruno, with his connections, might be of some help in this regard. Elke said she did not want to ask any favors from Bruno; he would demand some favors from her if he were to give her help in any way. I suggested *I* be the one to approach Bruno and they both reluctantly agreed it might be worth a try.

Dinner was over and it was still early so I figured this was as good a time as any; there was no use in delaying. I had bought a small bottle of what was supposed to be good Schnapps when we were shopping. I was going to replace the one that Gretchen had that was now empty. I decided to take that with me. I went down to the second floor of the "cell block" and found Bruno's door as he had described it. There was his name alongside the door and a bell under that. I noticed he also had a peephole in his door. I guess the Stasi's man in situ had a few extra perks that the other tenants did not. I rang the bell and stood in front of the peephole with my bottle of Schnapps visible and I hope what was a friendly, disarming look on my face.

I saw a shadow darken the peephole and then, the door was flung open. There was Bruno, hand outstretched and with a big smile on his face. "Ah, Herr Thomas," he said jovially. (I wondered who had told him my name. I know it wasn't the ladies or I.) "Gooten abend, good evening, my friend; it is so nice to see you again. May I be of some service to you?" "And a good evening to you also", I replied. "I have decided to take you up on your kind offer of assistance, Herr Hauptmann and see if perhaps you can advise me on how I should proceed in a certain matter." "My dear sir", he responded, "Nothing would give me greater pleasure. How can I help you?"

I explained that I had brought a small gift I hoped he would accept as a token of my gratitude for his help. I had been told, I said, that this was a good brand of Schnapps, I hoped I had not been mislead. With that, I handed him the bottle I had brought. He assured me it was a very superior brand then ushered me in and sat me in a comfortably upholstered chair in his living room. He said we must now share a glass of this most excellent Schnapps that I had brought. I could then tell him what had brought me to his door.

While Bruno was in another room fixing our drinks, I could look at my surroundings. Number one, it would appear that Bruno was not married and two, his furnishings were far superior to those in the apartment shared by Gretchen and Elke and I suspect, anyone else in the building. He had a telephone, a television set and a stereo system. His job with the Stasi must have paid quite well.

He returned shortly with the Schnapps and two small glasses on a tray that he deposited on the small table next to my chair and took the other chair next to it. He poured two glasses and when I pick up mine, lifted his and said, "Prosit, Herr Thomas, now tell me how I can help you." I explained that I was married to Frau Groenwald's niece and lived with her in California. (I had a sneaking suspicion that was something he already had found out.) My wife had not had any contact with her relatives for a long time and she had sent me to meet them and to check on their wellbeing. I was to take them for a visit to Frau Groenwald's sister-in-law, who lived in England and whom I had just recently met, for a few days holiday. First, however *I* must go to Switzerland to take care of some business of my own. I told him as it has become painfully apparent that I was not sufficient conversant in the language to properly take of what I must do, I had persuaded my wife's cousin, Elke, to act as my interpreter. I said I thought it best to send Frau Groenwald on ahead to her Sister-in-law to await our arrival as soon as my business was taken care of. I said that in my ignorance, I had forgotten they must have passports in order for me to do the things I had planned and I found now I was totally at a loss as to how to proceed, as were the ladies. I said, "I don't know if this is something with which you can help me, Herr Hauptmann but you do appear to be a very knowledgeable person and I am hoping you can give me some sound advice."

"Ah, Herr Thomas, my friend," he replied. "I do think it possible I may be able to help you but first I must make some investigation to determine how to do this in the best way possible. It may be necessary for me to pay certain fees however to expedite this transaction, which could otherwise take some weeks to complete. If you can advance me one hundred American dollars I can start tomorrow and find out what must be done." I had expected something like this and had brought some cash with me. I had just a little more than the amount he asked in my pocket. Best that he think he has gotten most of my ready cash. I tried to give that impression as I counted it out for him. I have no doubt more will be required before we finish with this transaction.

Bruno said he should have a progress report tomorrow. Why did I not stop by tomorrow evening and he would tell me how things were progressing. I promised that I would do that and trudged back up to the apartment to report to the ladies what had transpired. I told them I thought they were right, our friend Bruno was probably very well connected. He had found out my name. I just hope he does not learn I had been involved in the demise of certain people at least some of whom might have also been Stasi members.

I mentioned to the ladies that I almost wished I had some king of weapon. I was beginning to have an uneasy feeling. They glanced at each other and Gretchen nodded to her daughter who got up and left the room. When she returned, she handed me something wrapped in an oiled cloth. When I had it unwrapped, I found I was holding a German Army P38, fully loaded. With Elke's assistance, Gretchen explained that her husband had been in the Wehrmacht. He had taken this from a fallen officer around the time of the fall of Berlin. They had kept it hidden. If it had been found in their possession, they could have been in big trouble. They also had a few extra cartridges, if I needed them. I said most likely they would not be necessary but it was nice to know we were not defenseless should trouble develop. That P38 is a nice pistol. It was a replacement for the Luger which to my mind was even better but more expensive to manufacture. A few German officers had lugers but the great majority was issued the P38.

The next morning at breakfast, I told the ladies that as soon as we finished eating I must go back to the west zone again and make some telephone calls. I didn't want to risk making them from anywhere in this neighborhood. I expected to be back by lunchtime. If anyone asked, I had gone back for more groceries and would have something in my possession to back up that story.

I went back to the market I had visited several days ago with Elke. I had seen they had a public telephone. I bought a few things, including another bottle of Schnapps for Gretchen's pantry and wandered around the store for a while trying to see if anyone might be following me or have an interest in what I was doing. When it did not appear there was, I went to the phone and using my calling card, put through a call to the Roadrunner. It seemed to take hours but the call went thru and luckily, Elaine was still there. I told her I needed to phone Al for some advice and she gave me his office and his home phone numbers. I said, "Oh, by the way, are you two still *semi*-engaged?" I could hear her sputtering and then she said, "Of course we are, you nut; what did you expect? That young man knows when he has a good thing." I told her then I was in a bit of a rush right now and couldn't call Grethel; please tell her that I love her and to take good care of my humorous child. Then I said, "Bye now Elaine," and quickly hung before she could say, numerous.

Al was working late and I got him at his office. I told him what I had found out to date and then told him I was a little suspicious about my friend, Bruno Hauptmann. He was a known former Stasi informer and he seemed to have been checking on me as he knew things about me that I knew neither I or the ladies had told him. I hoped to be on my way to continue my investigations as soon as I could get Elke's mother on her way to England. I was awaiting passports for them the issuance of which was being expedited by my good friend Bruno. So far, I said, I don't think he is suspicious of me. Did he know who over here was following up on the information we had uncovered in Reno? If he did, did he think it would be all right if I contacted them if I found it necessary? He said he would have the information for me tomorrow. I told him I didn't know for sure what time I could phone and if he was not at the office would try him at home. If he spoke with Grethel, please assure her I was not doing anything she need worry about. Her cousin, Elke, was going along to act as my interpreter and would no doubt keep me out of any trouble. I took my purchases and headed back to the cellblock.

I went back to see what information Bruno had for me that evening after dinner. He cordially invited me in and insisted we share a drink; he had Bourbon or Scotch. I said Scotch would be just fine and he left to prepare drinks. He had nice soft music on his stereo tonight. His apartment was most attractive. Over drinks, he told me that yes, he was going to be able to get the passports we needed but to expedite the process that usually took over a month he must pay the clerks doing the processing for their extra work. Could I manage three hundred American dollars? "Hm", I mused, "You think that much, eh?" I pretended to be in thought then said that yes, I thought I could manage that by the time all the documents were ready. He said that would be just grand. He would inform the parties concerned to start work immediately. I told him I really did appreciate his assistance. I was anxious to complete all my errands here and return to my family as soon as possible.

He told me he could understand how I must be anxious to return to such an attractive wife. California must be a wonderful place in which to live. Maybe he would be able to visit California one of these days himself. As I prepared to leave, he said he expected to have the passports in a week and he would let me know when they were ready.

Now, how did he know I had an attractive wife or was he just guessing and *in California*? I can't figure out if he is letting me know he has been able to check up on me or if he had just inadvertently let the information slip out in our conversations. I must be careful and watch myself. It could be that I am just the source of a little extra income but right now, I cannot be sure. It was also possible he was determined somehow to get Elke for himself and wanted to be sure she did not get out of his reach; most likely both. Maybe also he could be finding out more about my recent activities than I wanted him to know. I must reach Al tomorrow and see what he can tell me.

CHAPTER SEVEN

WELL, WHAT DO YOU know? It was necessary we must return some of the clothing the ladies bought that were the wrong size or color. (The best excuse I could think of.) Gretchen and Elke both thought that was just a great idea. Until I had come, they had never had the opportunity to see the clothes the ladies in the free world had been enjoying for so long. We made a big production of it right after breakfast, dragging some of the clothes down to the car I had brought around to the front of the cellblock. As before, we went to the busiest store on the Tauensteinstrasse. It was now near lunchtime, as good a time as any for my purposes, I thought. The ladies knew what I intended and as they were busy wandering around the various racks I made my way out the rear exit of the store and slipped outside. Adjacent to the store was the rear door of a cozy appearing bar/café I had noticed the last time we were here. At least that is what it looked like. I entered the dim cool interior.

Inside I ordered a glass of lager and then wandered over to the telephones in the hallway by the restrooms. Good, no one else was using the phones and I dragged out my trusty calling card and dialed the about one hundred numbers necessary to reach Al. The call finally went through and Al said he had been anxiously awaiting my call. He did not have much time but listen: Tomorrow I should take the ladies to the Tiergarten. I would find a contact near the zoo. According to his contacts, I should be very careful of my good friend Bruno; he may not be exactly what he seemed to be. Al told me he was juggling two other important calls then and said he was sorry to have to leave me. Hmm, that is very interesting is it not?. I quietly slipped back into the store and into one of the comfortable chairs near the fitting rooms, which the management had thoughtfully provided for the husbands, boyfriends, etc. waiting for their ladies to make decisions. Why do not all stores do that?

While I was in the café, I had made a reservation for a table for lunch. As it was now near that time, the ladies concluded their transactions and I furnished my credit card to cover the additional charges. We left by the front entrance of the store and then went in the front entrance of the café next door. Our table was ready. If anyone checked, it was obvious why I had been in the cafe earlier. We had a nice lunch, which I said we certainly deserved. I had a glass of Scotch in advance; the ladies each had a glass of red wine of some kind. I wanted some more of that Sauerbraten with sweet and sour red cabbage and potato pancakes but it was not on the menu that day. It was a house specialty they said and took some time to prepare. It was only available on Wednesday and Saturday, sorry. Gretchen suggested a substitute, which turned out to be eminently satisfactory. I'm afraid I am going to get fat over here. While we ate, I said I thought I really should see the Tiergarten before I left Berlin. I had heard much about the zoo and the famous Schloss Schonbrunn. How about tomorrow, what did they think? Wunderbar! They had not been there since its restoration, after the war. They were in the wrong zone. They were really looking forward to our excursion.

In the car on the way home, I explained why I really wanted to go to the Tiergarten the next day. Now they were both worried. They had been worried about Bruno for a long time, partly because of his seeming obsession with Elke but a.lso because they knew of his Stasi connection and people were always wary of such people. The said informers were not always men either and one could never be too careful about their associates. The new government had not yet decided what to do about the now inactive Stasi or State Security Police as they were officially named. and their network of informers. They were both looking forward to getting away from Germany for a while. I hadn't told them I was going to try and see that absence was permanent.

We left on our excursion mid-morning. I cautioned them that we must now all seem to be happy and carefree. We were after all on a little holiday, were we not? I said furthermore when we returned we must not talk about any of our plans. I had no doubt that Bruno could have the apartment bugged if he thought it advisable. As far as anyone must know Gretchen was going to visit her sister-in-law for a brief holiday.

Elke would be joining her there shortly. They both expected to be returning sometime in the following month.

Well, the Tiergarten was interesting and we were all really enjoying out outing. As we neared the zoo, I noticed a kiosk selling coffee and sweet rolls. I thought it looked worthy of a closer look and took the ladies over to it and bought us all coffee. The smiling server said to the ladies in German that their friend appeared to be an American. If so, he would like to meet him. He was always interested in meeting people from other counties. Elke happily introduced me and our server said in English, as he surreptitiously palmed a small wad of paper into my hand, "It is indeed a pleasure to meet you Deputy Thomas. I hope you are enjoying your visit to our famous Tiergarten. If you can visit the famous Schloss later, Guide number seven is most knowledgeable and for a modest fee will give you a personally guided tour that I believe you will find most interesting." I thanked him and as we finished our coffee, we proceeded over to visit the zoo.

It was obvious we had found the contact that we were meant to. I knew Elke could not have introduced me as a deputy as she did not know I had been one. Obviously also, our friend knew exactly who I was. Now we must go to the Schloss in a little while and see if we can find this guide number seven. Gretchen and Elke were soon engrossed with the animals in the zoo and having a great time, which was good for our cover. I could hardly wait however to find out what guide number seven was going to show us. I stood it for an hour however and then insisted I just *had* to see the famous Schloss. Although I wanted to hurry, we strolled leisurely as though we had nothing more on our minds than to enjoy our visit.

While were in the zoo I had looked at the piece of paper the kiosk attendant had given me. It read, "Bruno Hauptmann is not informer but former Stasi higher-up. He is believed to have been responsible for the deaths of a number of people. One of the letters in the Reno collection was from him. Imperative you visit Schloss. Burn or swallow this. Thank goodness, it was a *little* scrap; I rolled it into a tiny ball and popped it into my mouth with the last of my coffee. I was sure no one had observed me.

We saw several uniformed guides when we entered the Schloss, all of them were guiding individual groups. Shortly after the last of these passed us, another guide appeared and approached us. He had a badge with the number seven on his coat. I had already noticed that none of the other guides had badges or numbers. When he saw that I had noticed his badge, our guide took the badge off and put it in his pocket. He said then, "I see your party has just missed the last tour group. If you wish, however I will be pleased to give you a tour of Schloss Schonbrunn; as you see I speak English and will be happy to provide translations where they may be required for our visitor from California." OK, he had let us know that he was he was the right one.

As we followed our guide and viewed the wonders of the palace, I noticed that the other tour groups were getting farther and farther ahead of us. Finally, as the group in front of us went around a corner, our guide stopped, opened a door next to us and ushered us inside. We were in a large ornate room. We crossed that and then entered another. There was a desk in that room with a number of comfortable chairs. There was a man sitting behind the desk who rose as we entered. He nodded to our guide who said, "No difficulties, Sir." He quickly took of the guides uniform coat and changed into another that matched his trousers, His small mustache was gone as well as the guide's cap he had been wearing. It happened so fast I almost didn't see it. I don't think the ladies had even noticed. I was impressed and told him so. He just smiled and said it was just part of the job.

The man standing behind the desk said that if we didn't mind their names would remain confidential for now, why not just call him, "Bob?" Just to be on the safe side could I tell him Al's last name? I said I knew him as Alfred R. Clarke, spelled with an "E" on the end. Unless she had come to her senses, he was engaged to marry one Elaine C. Mora. He laughed then and said that was Al all right. No one thought he was ever going to get married. I told him that Elaine would have convinced the most hardened bachelor that marrying her was the one thing he most wanted to do in this world and the sooner the better.

He invited us all to be seated then and then explained briefly to the ladies how we had uncovered the scheme that would get some people likely to be prosecuted for war crimes out of Europe, into the US. and given new identities before they could be prosecuted here. Some of these people were now already in custody in various jurisdictions here in Europe. There were others being sought. Some others were currently under investigation. Bruno Hauptmann was one of these although he didn't know it yet. He went on to elaborate then on how some of these people had been operating in California setting up their network when I had discovered their plan. FBI Agent Clarke had told them Deputy Thomas had been responsible for the demise of a number of these people who had made the mistake of harming his fiancé and had referred to me as a one-man army. Elke had been translating for her mother. I had not told any of these details to the ladies and they were both looking at me now with amazement on their faces. I told them that all this was really a gross exaggeration of what had happened. I had not played that important a part in all this.

The agent we were talking to, I assume he was CIA said he had been instructed by Agent Clarke to inform me that, as he had requested, Chief Deputy Miller had placed me back on active duty. He assumed I still had my badge and identification with me. In addition, also as requested, I was hereby detached and assigned to the FBI to serve at their pleasure. "As you know" Bob, continued," the FBI cannot operate outside of the country. Agent Clarke has arranged therefore that you be "loaned" to our agency. That is of course if you would agree."

Well, Holy Cow! Grethel will kill me if she hears of this. Finally, I said, "Well OK, Bob, if everyone will swear that my wife will never ever hear of this I'm on. As it was, she was very, very reluctant to have me leave California. I might never ever even get out of the house after this if she were eve to find out about this. Bob laughed and said they would do their best to keep my part in whatever developed super secret. He said I would be happy to know my pay would be exactly the same that I had been getting. I said that was a relief that at least it hadn't been reduced seeing I had been an unpaid volunteer. Bob chuckled and said that was one of the things that made me so valuable, as well as desirable. I was less of a strain on their budget. The Agency would however cover all my expenses and would give me an advance on those before I left. As I expect these might amount to more than just a little, that is certainly going to help me out.

I said, "Well OK, Bob, actually what I came here for was to find out what has happened to Grethel's father. He was last seen being taken from the jail in Austria where had been in custody. The Stasi had gotten an expedited Extradition Order and taken him away. As you no doubt know, he had become involved in this scheme that you are now investigating. Perhaps unwittingly, I am not yet sure. Now that you have told me about friend Bruno, I should point out that a year and a half ago Gretchen's husband was picked up by the Stasi who claimed he was an enemy of the state based on the statements he had been making, criticizing the Communist government; he was subsequently convicted of that and sent to prison. Shortly thereafter, Gretchen was informed, he had died in an accident in the prison laundry. Gretchen and Elke lost their home and Bruno had then arranged for them to move into the less than pleasant apartment, which the government had then assigned them. It was located in the same apartment building in which Bruno also resided although Bruno lived in much more pleasant circumstances."

I went on to speculate that now that I had discovered Bruno's apparent obsession with Grethel I was wondering if this might now be part of a plan of his. With her father dead and with she and her mother living now in such wretched circumstances, perhaps Elke might then be forced to succumb to his advances.

As Elke translated for her mother, they both had horrified looks on their faces. This thought had never occurred to them. They now appeared sure that Bruno must have been the one who had engineered their husband and father's disappearance. They were both weeping. Elke, when she could speak, said, "We never even saw who took him away. It was Bruno, who told us what had happened and then said how very sorry for us he was. He would do anything he could to help us he said. He did that by moving us into that wretched apartment in his building. I will kill him if I get the chance. He may have personally killed my father. At the least he arranged for it to be done."

I said, "Now Elke, you must be careful; we don't have proof this is what happened. So far, this is just an educated guess *on my part.*" Gretchen had not said a word while Elke had been interpreting. If Bruno could see the expression in her eyes, however he might be just a tad nervous. Probably not, I suspect old Bruno could handle himself pretty well. The Stasi were on a par with the KGB, with whom they had been closely allied. There were many who claimed that the Stasi were even more ruthless than was their counterpart in the USSR.

I said we must assume that by now Bruno may have some suspicion of me if only because he senses the possibility I may be going to put Elke out of his reach. I said I thought he likely will come through with the passports. I pointed out he had not asked for the necessary photos or information that goes in those documents. We can only assume that he had already had all that information in his possession. It would not surprise me. We can only hope he believes that we have no suspicions *of him*. If this does not work out maybe Bob here could get us documents that will get the ladies out of the country. I am sure Bruno is expecting that most likely Gretchen will fly to England and that Elke and I will take a plane to Switzerland. I had been making plans based on that assumption.

"This is what I had planned", I continued, "If Bob here will help me. As soon as I have all the passports, I will make the flight reservations. We will all leave on the same day that Gretchen leaves for England. She will depart first. When she is safely away, Elke and I will depart. With Bob's help, this is what I propose: After we see that Gretchen is safely off, Elke and I will go into the bar and linger over a drink or something to eat until our flight is called. When that happens I will suggest to Elke that maybe we should quickly use the restroom facilities before we embark. This is where we need Bob's expert assistance. This time of the year, almost everyone is wearing a coat and a hat. If Bob can arrange to have two people in the restrooms of the same general appearance as Elke and I, Immediately as we enter them we will exchange coats and hats and in Elke's case, purses and immediately leave and proceed to the front entrance of the terminal. We will proceed as strangers to each other and proceed separately to the outside. At the exchange of hats and coats we will hand our plane tickets to our replacements, they will have to hurry, and board the plane for their free all expense paid trip to Switzerland.

"Now, Bob", I continued, "If you can have a car out front we can use. Elke and I will manage to meet there. I intend to take the autobahn to Dresden and won't be wasting any time either. From there I will continue south to the Czech Republic. That will get us out of Germany the quickest way possible. Assuming I don't get lost somewhere, we will continue south into Austria. I will try to pick up the trail of Grethel's father there and if unsuccessful there, will then proceed on to Switzerland to check the bank accounts he had there to see if he might have accessed them. That is as far as I have been able to plan things so far. One thing that bothers me is not having any protection. Gretchen has offered me her husband's P38 but I am reluctant to take that as I have no permit and if we were to be stopped, we might be in some serious trouble. Now, I would really appreciate the comments of you gentlemen and any suggestions you may have about what I have outlined. Does it sound to you like a plan that is workable?"

"Well, Deputy Thomas," Bob said, "I guess maybe Al was right when I asked him for his assessment of you. He said I was not to let your unassuming appearance fool me. I think your plan is a good one and we will have enough time to get all the necessary people and things we need in place. If you can somehow let me know when you intend to appear at the airport to make your reservations, I will try to contact you there if it appears safe to do so". Then he gave me a phone number on a scrap of paper. I pointed out then that we had been here for some time now and we should be on our way before someone might notice what we were doing. As we walked out, I cautioned the ladies to have a pleasant expression, just as if we had just been having a pleasant tour and were now on our way home or perhaps for something to eat. Smile and chat.

We did all that and eventually made our way back to Stalag Number Nine and our beds. All three of us were tired out. It had been a mentally exhausting time for all of us. As I was dropping off to sleep, I could hear Elke and her mother talking. I knew what they were discussing. They had some new and shocking ideas to consider.

CHAPTER EIGHT

WELL, BRUNO HAS HAD a week to produce the passports. It's time for me to find out if he is going to have them as promised. I decided that to night, after dinner, would be as good a time as any to check with him and find out. One thing about him he always seems to be home. Tonight turned out to be no exception and as usual, he greeted me with a jovial smile and handshake and invited me into his apartment. He informed me, as we had our ritual drink, that yes, he had been assured he would have all the necessary documents in two days. I told him how I really appreciated his assistance. I really was anxious to finish my business in Europe and return to my home. I would go to the bank to morrow and arrange for the money to pay him for his services when he could deliver the passports to me. I said, "Of course, my friend Bruno, I am assuming that everything is going to be strictly legitimate. I certainly don't want to wind up having a lot of trouble." He assured me all be perfectly correct, as I would see. As I was leaving, I told him then that if all was he had told me, I might ask that he could do me another small favor before we left. He said that to do so would be his pleasure. He was sure that when he could come to California I would surely do as much for him. (Hmm; now is that a slip or is he doing this on purpose?)

I was at the main branch of the Dresdner Bank AG, in the formerly west sector, by ten the next morning. I presented my Platinum American Express Credit Card and explained that I needed one thousand dollars in American money, seven hundred to be in fifty-dollar denominations and the rest, one hundred dollar bills. They assured me all would be ready for me the next afternoon anytime before closing time. When I asked, was there was a phone on which I could make a private local call, I was ushered to a small office and left there to my own devices.

The number Bob had given me answered on the first ring with

a simple, "hello". I asked to speak to Bob and he came on the line immediately. I told him that Bruno expected to have the passports tomorrow and I had arranged to pick up the money in American dollars to pay him tomorrow afternoon. I told him the bank I was using and he said he would meet me there at two o'clock when I arrived to pick up the money. Luckily, Bruno was coming out of the building just as I returned to the apartment. Good, that saved me another trip up to his apartment. I told him I had just arranged with the bank for the Money in American Dollars as he had requested and would pick it up to morrow if the bank did as they had said. He said he was delighted and he would check again today. He wanted to be sure that everything could be delivered to me tomorrow as he had promised.

That night Gretchen has a surprise for me at dinner. First, I had to sit and have a small glass of Kirshwasser. I swear, it must have been about 800 proof, in any event it sure did clear ones sinuses. Next, I sat at the table with my eyes closed until given the OK to look. My, what heavenly aromas were wafting from the kitchen! Finally, I was allowed to look and there before me was my now favorite dinner: sauerbraten, sweet and sour red cabbage and potato pancakes. Gretchen had been working on that for three days to surprise me. What a nice lady she is!

I declare, I must have feasted forever, at any rate it seemed I had. What a delicious meal! I told Gretchen that it was a good thing for her that I was already married or I would steal her away for sure. I could see when Elke translated for her, that she was pleased. At any rate, she gave my arm a little push and said something like, "Oh, go along with you now", or whatever it is they would say in German. I find that although I don't always understand the words exactly I can often figure out what they mean.

The ladies went with me to the bank the next morning. They decided they must replace certain of their personal things with items that they wanted to take with them. We would do that when I finished at the bank. I told them, as we were driving to the bank, that they should take all their good things with them and leave everything else. They didn't really have that many good things. After all, they would be returning soon anyway, nicht vahr? (I hope that means, "right?")

The ladies were seated in comfortable chairs in the lobby while I was ushered into the same little office where I had made my phone call the day before. Bob was waiting there with an assistant manager who was handling my transaction. I was surprised that he spoke English like an American until he explained that he was from the bank's New York office and was here to perfect his German and to learn more of their European operation. The bank did the same with their European employees and sent some of them to England and America to perfect their language skills and observe how banking was done in those locations. Bob whispered that the assistant manager was also an "assistant" of his. I understood. The money I requested had been divided into four small envelopes so I could distribute them about my person more easily. As I prepared to leave, I told Bob I would be at the airport the next morning at ten o'clock to make my reservations. He said he would see me there.

I took the ladies back to their favorite store and after going next door to make a dinner reservation, returned and sat in the back while they did their shopping. I should be getting the volume rate at the restaurant if we eat there many more times. Later, over dinner, we went over our plans in detail for our departure until I was sure everyone knew just exactly how it was to be carried out. We could no longer risk discussing our plans in the apartment.

We were back at the apartment by early evening. Well I guessed it was now or never and made my way down to Bruno's apartment. He was expecting me, greeted me in his usual jovial manner, and insisted I come in and be comfortable. We should of course share a small Kirshwasser to celebrate this occasion should we not? He handed me all the documents and insisted I examine them carefully so I could assure myself that they were indeed genuine. Of course I really wouldn't know if they were genuine or not but at any I rate peered at them closely. Actually, they looked pretty good to me. I counted out the three hundred dollars then and handed them over thanking him profusely for his assistance.

I said then, "You know, Bruno, we will be leaving shortly. The ladies are concerned about their apartment and their possessions while they are going to be away. I was wondering if I might hire you for a month to keep an eye on their apartment and possessions as I know it would ease their minds to know someone was keeping an eye on things while they were away. I would of course expect that you should be compensated if you could do this for me. Would one hundred dollars, American, be enough to compensate you for your time? If so, I will have the money for you before I leave for Switzerland."

My gosh, for minute I thought he might be going to kiss me. "My dear sir", he gushed, "You may rely on me to the utmost. It will be my very great pleasure to be of service to the fraulein and her mother. It will also be my great pleasure to welcome them on their return. We shook hands and I went back upstairs to let the ladies know that Bruno had agreed to guard their possessions. There were overjoyed and expressed themselves joyously. If Bruno has the place bugged, as I suspect, I hope he picks that up. Maybe I should open up an acting school when we finish all this. I hope he is now convinced that Elke will be coming back and will not be escaping whatever it is he has planned. We still must be very careful. I suspect Bruno is a slippery old devil.

Chapter Nine

I WAS NEARING THE Lufthansa counter at the airport the next morning when a uniformed clerk approached me. He said, "You may step over here, sir, I am just opening this window for reservations." It was Bob. We went through some ritual but everything had already been taken care of and the tickets were ready for me. He said all was in readiness as we had planned. I would recognize guide number seven as soon as I entered the restroom. They had an agent who looked much like Elke although perhaps not quite as attractive, waiting in the ladies restroom. She will be wearing or carrying a tan trench coat. have on a large black hat and carrying a large black shoulder bag. The bag will contain many things we are going to need so be careful of it. There are visas for the Czech Republic and Austria, a permit from Interpol for the Glock in the bottom of the bag and phone numbers in Prague, Salzburg, Innsbruck and Zurich, should I need them. Just ask for Bob. Could I remember the name he asked me, with a slight grin.

As I exit, I should look for a green Audi out in front. A porter wearing a number seven badge will be standing by it. We can't keep buying badges with different numbers you know," he said with another smile. "When you tell him you are the Deputy, he will hand you the car keys. By then it is to be hoped that Elke will have joined you. If you leave your luggage in the rental car when you turn it in, we will see that it is transferred to the Audi.

There are two sets of license plates on the car. After you cross the Czech border and, when you can reach a proper place, stop and remove the top set of plates and place them in the boot. (That is trunk to you, Deputy.) There is some Austrian and some Swiss money in with the tickets. If you run short, phone good old Bob at one of those numbers. And—for goodness sake, don't forget to give the plane tickets to your replacements. Now--do have a good trip, Sir." He shook my hand as he handed me an envelope. Gollee! I hope I remember all that.

The ladies had been waiting in the lobby while I concluded my business and we now decided to have lunch at my favorite café and discuss our plans; rats, still no volume rate and worse, not a sauerbraten day. Not my lucky day I guess. As we ate, I went over all the things Bob had told me on how things we supposed to be done to morrow. Then I suggested to Elke that in the morning she start wearing her hair up and then let it down when she and the agent traded hats. She thought that would be a good idea. It looked like there was nothing more to discuss so we headed on back to the apartment to pack for our journey tomorrow. Everyone was so keyed up no one was very hungry at dinnertime. I barely was able to finish the sauerbraten left over from last night's dinner.

Well, it was time to do my last chore and so I made my way down to our friend Bruno's apartment. After our obligatory drink, I told him we were leaving tomorrow and I had the one hundred dollars that I had promised. I told him again how much I appreciated his taking the time to safeguard the apartment for Frau Groenwald and Elke in their absence. He assured me that to do so would give him great pleasure and assured me of his undying friendship. He hoped someday soon to see me in California. Who knows, he might even be bringing a lady friend with him. (Lots of luck, Bruno.)

We had been instructed to be at the airport an hour ahead of time. I had to turn in the rental car and sign the credit card slips to cover the charges so we started even earlier. We had been too excited and keyed up to have any appetite for breakfast so we started out soon after the ladies had finished getting all their makeup applied to their satisfaction. As planned, Elke's and my luggage were left in the rental. We just had small carry-on bags and Gretchen's luggage to take into the terminal and check with the agent at the Lufthansa ticket counter. I suggested then that we have coffee and a sweet roll while we waited and the ladies agreed. It was difficult to sit there and chat, and smile while we waited for what seemed like hours for Gretchen's flight to finally be called but we did just that.

It was finally time for Gretchen to board and we all walked casually to the boarding area to see her off, laughing and chatting as if this was the most ordinary of occasions. There were "bon voyage" wishes and kisses and hugs exchanged and she proceeded finally into the aircraft. We watched until the airplane was out of sight. I had been casually gazing about the airport from time to time since we had first arrived at the terminal. If anyone had any interest in us, it surely was not apparent to me, however, if such a person were a real pro we never would have noticed them anyway. I hope I am not getting paranoid about possibly being under surveillance.

It was another fifty minutes before the flight to Switzerland was scheduled and the board said it was on time. As planned, Elke and I sat in the little bar just off the boarding area, nursed a drink, and pretended to be chatting as we waited for our flight to be called. We both were a bit nervous I knew but I don't really believe we gave any outward signs of that. Lufthansa flight 405 to Bern, Vienna and Budapest was announced and we put our agreed plan into action. There he was, guide number seven, waiting just inside the entrance to the restroom. Fortunately, it was empty except for us. He immediately clapped a hat on my head as he put mine one his, he skillfully applied a small mustache on me as I slipped on his overcoat. I handed him the plane ticket turned around and left. Amazing! It took no more than two minutes, even better than I had thought possible.

I didn't walk too fast as I made for the exit as I had not seen Elke as yet. I suspect it would take a trifle longer for her to make the change than it did me. As I neared the exit I glanced idly about again and it now .looked like she was on her way. At any rate, a blond in a tan coat and black hat was heading in my direction. OK' so far, so good.

Outside and a few yards down the street outside the exit stood a green car. There was a porter standing next to a pile of luggage on the sidewalk next to it. As I got nearer, I saw he was wearing a badge on his uniform jacket with the number seven. He appeared to be looking past me but I knew he was watching me. I pretended to be looking elsewhere also. I just couldn't resist; as I was just alongside I whispered out of the side of my mouth: "Hello there Double O Seven, Deputy Bond here; James Bond, that is." He couldn't help but snicker as he handed me a set of car keys. He told me the doors were unlocked and proceeded to load the luggage into the trunk, I mean boot.

I could see Elke now. She was walking toward me with a slightly bewildered look. Ah, she didn't recognize me. The mustache must have fooled her. Good, maybe it would anyone else that might have been looking for me as well. As she reached me I raised my hat politely and inquired, "Miss Greenwood, is it not? Perhaps I may offer you transportation." She had caught on immediately and answered, "You are very kind, sir. It would indeed be of assistance if you can provide me with transportation." I made it obvious I was tipping the porter and he ushered Elke into the passenger side of the car. I got in the driver's side and figured out how to get the thing started and in gear and we were on our way. We both heaved a sigh of relief. Now all we had to do was find our way to the Autobahn leading to Dresden.

I had noticed as I had gotten in the car that there was a handful of maps on the seat. I told Elke that I bet the top one showed the route to Dresden and the border crossing. She looked and sure enough, it did. That Bob was one thoughtful guy. I asked Elke if she had remembered to give her replacement the plane ticket and she said she had. She had been so nervous and excited that she had actually forgotten but her replacement had reminded her at the last minute. She hoped she hadn't made any other mistakes. We had about one hundred fifty miles to cover and we should do that in about three hours or less at the speeds they drove these Autobahns. As soon as we got to a place to pull off I was going to do that so we could examine the black bag Elke was carrying. We had soon actually gotten on the correct road and were now well on our way.

In about an hour, we reached a place that provided gasoline, food and restroom facilities. We had a full tank to start with but I topped off the tank and then pulled into a parking space. I got each of us a coffee and then we opened up the black bag to see what we had.

Right on top was a letter of instructions. We were informed there was a nine-millimeter Glock in the bottom of the bag plus some spare ammo. The permit with it was issued to a Deputy William Thomas of the Inyo County Sheriff's Office and issued by the Interpol office in Paris. There was also a cell phone. That was supposed to be good almost anywhere in Europe, There were various visas should we need them. There was a packet of American money in tens and twenties. Whenever possible, I should contact Bob at the numbers I had been given, when in those particular cities; for sure if I came across any information relating to Bob's ongoing investigation.. I would find pliers and a screwdriver in the glove box. Please don't forget to take the top plate off as we had discussed. OK, time to be on our way.

We didn't have much to talk about. That was partly because I really had to pay attention to my driving. There was a lot of traffic and as we got nearer to Dresden, it became quite heavy. Dresden is one of the largest cities in Germany and we arrived there shortly after noon. It appeared half the population must be out in their cars going to or from lunch. Elke had been looking for us to get something to eat and found a likely looking place shortly after we had cleared the worst of the traffic. I gotta tell you; I do not like driving in Europe. These damn *foreigners* drive like maniacs.

After a quick sandwich and a cup of coffee, we were on our way. In a few more minutes, we were at the border with the Czech Republic. This was something new to both of us. I guess we were both nervous as we waited in the line of cars going through the checkpoint. Finally, it was out turn. The guard at my widow said politely, "passports bitte." So far, I could handle this. I handed him my American and Elke's German passports'. He opened them and scanned them carefully. I knew mine was OK but I wasn't sure whether Bruno may have managed to trick me. The guard looked across at Elke and started speaking. Then he was smiling. Elke was giving him a shy smile as she nodded her head and replied. They were talking so fast I couldn't understand a word. Finally, with a laugh and a few final words he waved us ahead. The Czech border guards looked as us as we slowed down and then waved us right on through. I guess they figured that if the German guards were going to pas us we were OK.

That was easier than I expected. When I asked Elke what all the conversation was about her face was a little pink and she said she would explain when we stopped to change the plates. It was about twenty minutes later that we came to a small town and I pulled off the highway and found a place where I could change the plates unobserved. I did that as quickly as possible and got us back on the highway. Elke had the next map out and it covered this country. We would stay on this highway all the way to Prague. It did not seem to be much more than about a hundred miles, more or less, so we should be there by early afternoon. I think that is as far as I want to go for today. So far, it has been a pretty exciting day.

I asked Elke if it was all right with her if we stopped here for the night and she said we should. She said that she realized I was on a mission but Prague was an ancient and interesting city and it would be a shame not to see a little of it. Obviously, she had never been here before or anywhere else for that matter and likely would not have another chance to see it. Maybe we could see some of the famous places such as the St..Vitus Cathedral before we resumed our journey. I said of course, why hadn't I thought of that. Now she was very happy. Her movements had been greatly restricted as she was growing up she and had never been on a holiday of any sort.

As we neared the city, I asked Elke to be on the lookout for a policeman. There must be a tourist information office somewhere in the city where we could inquire about hotel accommodations. No doubt he would be able to give us direction on finding it.. She nodded and soon thereafter spotted one. Apparently, the people here speak German as she was having no difficulty. Now he too was laughing and pointing out on the map where we should go. He said something to me and I smiled and said, "Danke". I hope it was the right thing. Elke began chuckling then too.

Following Elke's directions, I had us at our destination in fifteen minutes. We went inside. I told Elke she had been doing so well and spoke the language so I would leave the negotiating to her. If we are going to try to see some of the sights, perhaps we might get something near enough that we might even walk to some of them tonight. The lady helping us asked Elke something and I noticed that same shy look again. The lady laughed, clapped her hands gleefully and then picked up the phone. I assume she was making a reservation for us. She wrote something on a piece of paper she handed to Elke and said something as she shook hands. She turned to me then said something, smiling broadly and shook hands with me also. If I ever finish the escapade, I'm only going where I understand what they are saying.

The hotel we needed was marked on our map and we were there in ten minutes. It looked like a nice place and did not look too expensive. We pulled up in front and the doorman came down and opened the car door for Elke. I guess she must have told him we had a reservation as he picked up a telephone by the door and talked to someone. Presently two porters or bellmen came out to our car. Elke said that if I would hand them the keys they would see to the transfer of our luggage and to garaging the car. OK, I can handle that. Having Elke has sure paid off up to now. I guess bringing her along as an interpreter has been a good idea.

We approached the sign-in desk where we were given comfortable seats. I presented our passports and signed the guest register where indicated. The manager spoke to Elke who answered and he broke out in a big smile and said something. Elke smiled and said "Danke". He has welcomed us to the hotel, Wilhelm," she told me "and hopes we will enjoy our accommodations."I said, "Thank you very much, Sir."He replied, "You are very welcome, Sir." Well, why didn't every one speak English before? We were then ushered to an old-fashioned elevator. The kind you have seen in some old movies. This was ornate with much gilded wrought iron. In it, we rose slowly and regally to our assigned floor. We were shown to our door. That was then unlocked by the bellman and the key presented to me as the door was opened with a flourish.

My, what a room, It was beautiful! From the window, which has a small balcony, you could see the river. What a marvelous view! I knew from our map it was the Vltava, which I guess is in the Czech language. The Germans I think called it the Moldau. I turned away from the view and saw the bellman standing next to the small table in the center of the room. On it there was a vase of pretty flowers and next to that what appeared to be a champagne bucket with what must be, of course, a bottle of champagne. My, they surely do treat their guests right at this establishment.

Elke asked me if I was ready to have the champagne opened and when I said it sounded like a good idea she said something to the bellman and he proceeded to do that. He soon had two flutes of champagne on a small tray, which he presented to us in turn. I figured I should give him a tip so he could depart so handed him one of the two five dollar bills I had. He was so effusive in his thanks I figured I had gone and over tipped again. He kept bowing as he backed out of the room and softly closed the door behind him.

As the door closed, I turned to Elke. "O.K., let's have it", I demanded. "How come we are getting the Royal treatment, Elke? Why do we have only one room? Tell me exactly, what is going on here? "Let us sit in those comfortable chairs by the window, William and sip our champagne," she said, "I will explain what has happened. I hope you will not be angry with me."

She went on to explain then how it had all started as we crossed the border that first time. The border guards just assumed we must be newly married and it was easier to let them think that than try to explain about an unmarried couple with passports from different countries traveling together. I had noticed, had I not, that they had barely looked at our documents after they had reached that conclusion? She chuckled when she told me that when the guard said he hoped that I would have many children, I had politely thanked him. The lady at the tourist office was so sure we were newlyweds that she went out of her way to find us the best accommodations and to alert the hotel of our special circumstances. "And that, my dear William is how you became a married man shortly after arriving in Germany." she concluded. "I do hope you are not angry with me." .

I told her that although she might look like Grethel, I knew without a doubt that Grethel would not tolerate her substituting for anything more than just her appearance. Although I agreed that although likely Elke had done the right thing under the circumstances, I feared that if Grethel were to learn what was happening I would be in serious trouble at home. Elke said then I should fear not, she would insure that my reputation would remain unsullied as far as she was concerned. She pointed out then that perhaps there might be some advantages, for the time being, if everyone *did* think we were husband and wife. Maybe we should think about that. I sure wish I could talk to Grethel.

Well, I wanted to talk to someone. I was supposed to telephone "Bob" when we got to the city anyway so likely this was as good a time as any. The phone was answered on the first ring. When I announced that it was Deputy Thomas for Bob, the local "Bob" was on the phone at once. He said he was glad I had phoned. We were to visit the famous St. Vitus Cathedral tomorrow. Around ten in the morning, someone would contact us. Be near the resting place of the Good King Wenceslas. He hung up. Well that was a short conversation and somewhat one-sided as well. Of course I had heard the Good King Wenceslas Christmas many times. It hadn't occurred to me that there had actually been such a person. When I relayed our instructions on to Elke she pointed out we had been going to the cathedral tomorrow anyway.

It was four o'clock now and we had not had much lunch or for that matter much of anything to eat today. I suggested it might be a nice time to walk down toward the river and maybe we would find some place down there to get something to eat. Elke said that was a good idea, she was hungry and suggested we check with the Concierge for some suggestions on a likely place. That sounded reasonable.

The Concierge knew who we were and went to great pains to welcome us to the hotel and to the city of Prague. He did all this in English, which was even better. I explained what we had in mind and he gave us what turned out to be easily followed directions. He assured us we would find a number of attractive cafes and restaurants near the Vltava. Then as we prepared to leave he said, "The hotel wishes to congratulate you on your wedding Herr and Frau Thomas. As is the custom of the hotel, for newlyweds who stay here, we wish to provide you a complimentary breakfast in bed. The waiter and his assistant will arrive at eight-thirty tomorrow morning. I am sure it is something you will enjoy. Please tell your friends. I stammered a "Thank you very much, Sir." and we left. Even Elke was somewhat nonplussed. Now how in the hell am I going to handle this? I swear, if I ever get home, I'll never leave California again. 'Might never even leave the house.

I guess there is nothing we can do about it for the present so we started out on our walk. For some reason I don't seem to be as hungry as I was just a short time ago. Maybe that will change when I get out into the open air. It seemed to have suddenly gotten very stuffy.

Elke took my arm as we started out and I guess we really must have given the appearance of a newly married couple as we strolled in the direction of the river. I suppose it *might* be a good idea, for the time being anyway, to give that impression. I know that perhaps I shouldn't be, but I am a little upset with Elke for getting me into this predicament. It does not seem to be a bother for her. I think that maybe she is just very happy to have gotten away from Bruno and the problems she was facing back in Berlin.

What an interesting city! Taking this walk was a good idea; there are so many interesting buildings in this part of the city. The tourist office lady had surely put us in a good location. Before long, we found a restaurant along the river that looked particularly inviting and decided to give it a try. We were a little early for the heavy dinner trade and so were able to get a table right by a window where we could look out over the river. What a picturesque sight, with boats on the river and the magnificent buildings that lined the shore. I told Elke I had decided this was a good time to have the first of my six or eight drinks. I was only kidding of course; two is usually my limit unless of course someone forces me. When our waiter found we had never been to the city before he was happy to tell us much of the history of this part of the city and the river. He was quite knowledgeable. We asked that he select a dinner for us and it turned out to be a most enjoyable experience with truly delicious food. He told us that it was obvious that we were just newly married and the restaurant wished us to enjoy a bottle of wine with our dinner with their complements.

What is going on with all these people? Why all of a sudden do we appear to be a newly married couple? Granted, Elke is unusually attractive but there must be something else going on I haven't been able to figure out. I am feeling uneasy about this; not enough however that I wasn't able to finish all of our delicious dinner. Well it was finally time to get back to the hotel. To tell the truth, it has been a rather long day. I think we are both getting tired now. Walking back through the bracing autumn air of the early evening with a pretty girl was very pleasant way to end the evening.

Now, to decide on our sleeping arrangements. Elke said she would trust me to share her bed, which, she pointed out, was actually quite large. I told her that seemed just a little risky to me. Make that much, much too risky. I said I would make do on the sofa, which also was large as well. I would move in with her when the breakfast tray arrived temporarily until the waiters had left. I was a married man and I was sure I would not feel right if I did not. Elke laughed and said she was going to tell Grethel, when they met, how she had to literally drag me into her bed. Gollleee! How in the world do I get myself into these situations? If Grethel and Elaine hear about this little episode, my life is going to be a living hell I am sure. Well the sofa turned out to be very comfortable and I was out like a light as soon as I was horizontal and covers up to my chin. Now-----you see what a clear conscience will do for you.

Elke was shaking me or I would have no doubt slept until noon. My, my, my, she was a sight to behold! She was wearing a beautiful negligee over her nightgown. Thank the lord; it was not one of those practically transparent ones such as Grethel drags out ever so often. Believe me; it was bad enough. If anyone were to see me in this situation, I know I could neverin this world, convince anyone of my total innocence. When she could see she had my attention Elke announced that it was almost eight o'clock; perhaps I might wish to make myself presentable before I went to bed with her. Yes, that is exactly the way she said it, chuckling all the while. It was stupid of me to have let her see how she could get me so flustered. She just delights in needling me now at every opportunity.

OK, I'm up, shaved, teeth brushed and hair combed. I guess I look as good as possible. To be on the safe side I had put on my underwear back on under the pajamas. I added a bathrobe on top of that. Elke began laughing so hard when I came into the room I thought she might have a stroke. I had forgotten I had put socks and shoes on also. Perhaps that is a bit much. I took them off. I was even convinced to lay the robe across the foot of the bed and for goodness sake, she said, please button up the top of the pajamas so the underwear does not show. I was about to give the whole show away. "Now," she asked, leering at me, "Are you ready for us to do our thing?" She burst out laughing again at my shocked expression.

It is just about that time, so I sort of snuck into the bed, sitting along the side. Elke plopped herself right in the middle and told me that if I didn't move next to her the staff would be spreading the word all over the hotel that the newlyweds were having their first spat. OK, I moved a little closer just as we heard a k nock on the door and the announcement that breakfast was about to be served. Elke immediately grabbed me around the waist, plastered me right against her, let her head rest on my shoulder and let her peignoir and gown slip well off her shoulder just as the waiter and his assistant came wheeling in the cart with our breakfast things. I can just see me now trying to convince anyone of my innocence, cant you?

Well first, there was a big wicker tray with short legs that was placed across our laps and then a beautiful breakfast began to be spread before us. The coffee smelled like ambrosia for the gods! I realized now, that despite the torture, Elke, had been putting me through, I was hungry. Everything looked absolutely delicious! The waiter and *the serving wench* then removed the cart with the announcement that *the serving wench* would return with more coffee and some freshly baked sweet rolls in a little while. I guess that was the gist of Elke's interpretation. Well, I sure was stuck in the bed for now. There was no way I could get out from under this big tray with all the food on it anyway. I started eating.

Elke gave me a squeeze then and said, "See William, that wasn't so painful was it?" I had to agree it was not but I did not think this was something a married man should be doing in a hotel bed with a beautiful woman that was not his wife. Elke said yes, she agreed that under normal circumstances what I was saying was very true however our circumstances definitely were not normal and undoubtedly we would have to improvise at times. Well, we started in then chatting, eating, and really enjoying this marvelous breakfast. Maybe we *shall* tell our friends as the Concierge asked.

As promised, after knocking, the young woman with the coffeepot returned with a basket of wonderful looking sweet rolls. While she was doing her chores, she and Elke began whispering together. I noticed her eyeing me surreptitiously from time to time and then, with an expression on her face that could only be construed as one of approval, she left. Elke said she would return for the tray when we finished eating. When I asked her why all the whispering she said it was just girl talk. I asked then why had the girl kept looking at me so strangely and she said OK then, she would tell me. It seems the staff, particularly the female portion, had been speculating at some length about how well an American man might perform his nuptial duties. "I finally told her Wilhelm", she said, "That you were just unbelievable." I think that was really a good choice of words, don't you? I guess you saw the look of approval. There should be just about enough time now for the word to have reached all who might have had an interest."

I told her, "Elke, you are a rat! You know their interpretation is going to be different from what you actually meant. No one is ever going to believe now that we are not in fact a newly married couple." Elke said that she believed that was something we were just going to have to live with and now we must get ready for our visit with Bob and Good King Wenceslas. Then she said, "Oh, as long as you seem reconciled with our marital situation, William, should we save time by taking our showers together? When she saw the shocked expression on my face, she doubled over with laughter again and when she could finally talk, added, "I guess from your expression that perhaps you are not quite ready for that yet." More laughter. Finally, "Please forgive me, William," she asked, "I just can't resist. You should see the expressions of terror and dismay on your face whenever I trick you like that. I promise not to tease you anymore----this morning." She laughed again. I want to go home.

The Concierge said we would find that the cathedral was within easy walking distance. As the weather was quite nice this morning, we decided to walk there. This also gave us the opportunity to view the baroque palaces and all the other interesting buildings along our route. You never saw so many steeples and spires. It made for a spectacular skyline indeed. We soon reached the cathedral and with time to spare. We wandered about observing the many interesting things there were to see. There were a number of other people doing the same thing. In another part of the vast nave, a religious service was taking place. It was getting close to the time of our meeting so I thought we should try to discover where the Good King might be interred.

Chapter Ten

I don't suppose we will find him standing around somewhere so perhaps it will be best if we can find a curator, church official or docent to help us. It was just a few minutes to the hour so we should be in the right place very soon.

We had been standing near one of the giant pillars in the cathedral, looking for someone who might give us directions, when a pleasant appearing young woman stepped out from behind it and began speaking to Elke, apparently in the Czech language. When Elke answered in German, she smiled and switched to that language. I guess it is not surprising that many Czechs speak German considering how long that Adolf had annexed the Sudetenland into the Third Reich. At the end of WWII, of course they had the opportunity to learn Russian when Joseph Stalin grabbed them off for the USSR. Now that they have regained their freedom, I suppose there a number of languages that can now be heard here, in addition to the official Czech language.

The only word I could make out from their conversation was, "Wenceslas". Apparently, Elke must be asking for directions to his place of entombment. I guess the lady must have asked Elke her name as I recognized that. I could tell by her tone of voice that she had asked, "and your friend?" I know freund is the German word for friend. I heard Elke give my name and with that, the lady came over to me, put out her hand and said, "I am happy to meet you, Deputy, my name is, " Bob." I told her she must be the best looking "Bob" I had seen in a long, long time. She laughed and said that if it would make me feel better I could call her Roberta. She then told us we would not have time to visit with the Good King today. There have been some important new developments that we must discuss, she said. It was best that we adjourn to a nearby café where we can do that. With that, we left the Cathedral, Roberta leading the way.

We soon found a nearby café and secured a secluded table. Roberta began with her news without further ado. It seems we may be going to have a problem. There had in fact been a watcher at the airport to keep tabs on us. He had followed us onto the airplane; at least he thought he had, until the plane landed in Switzerland and he discovered we had tricked him. Our friends in Berlin were sure that, so far, no one had any idea where we were. Bruno appears now to be a very unhappy camper. So much so that he has dreamed up a little scheme of his own.

He has filed a complaint with the police alleging that Elke tried to kill him when he discovered her trying to break into his apartment. He showed the holes he claims were from the bullets she fired that had barely missed him. Thanks to good old Bruno, there is now an arrest warrant out on Elke for burglary and attempted murder. She is believed to be somewhere in Germany as she obviously did not go to Switzerland. When no trace of her can be found in Germany, the police in the other countries of Europe will no doubt be notified.

In order to fill the ranks of the new police force in what was East Germany it was necessary the government recruit some who were former Stasi or border guards; trying to eliminate any of the worst of the lot. They had met only moderate success in that regard. Our people in Berlin are now concerned that if any of these people start digging, they may discover my connection to the investigation of the network we had uncovered in Reno. It now appears that some current and former Stasi members are heavily involved in the operation of the network or as potential users of the same. Doubtless, some of these people are aware of the role Grethel's father played in all this as well. If they discover that I have come here to find out what happened to him------------.

When you consider that all those countries formerly in the USSR had their own secret police until the whole thing went Kaput; there are likely a large number of people who may have been engaged in activities that are now likely to result in prison terms for them, if not something more dire. That means there could now be a large number of rather unpleasant people who would not wish to see a potential escape route denied them. I sure as hell don't want them all to be looking for me---or Elke either for that matter. A very pretty ballad comes to my mind that seems to fit this situation. (You do know I have been told I sing like a thrush, do you not?) About now, I should no doubt render a few bars of, "I guess I'll have to change my plans".

I told Roberta these new developments were going to require a little thought. I suggested that Elke and I return to the hotel so I could do that. Perhaps we could meet later somewhere where we could talk undisturbed. Roberta said, "Good idea, Deputy; *We* will pick you up in front of the hotel at seven-thirty.

Elke and I declined a ride. We didn't talk much as we strolled to the hotel. It was quite pleasant walking in the crisp fall air and with a very pretty girl holding your arm was even more so. I told Elke that and she gave my arm a friendly squeeze. I often think clearer while walking and by the time we had neared the hotel, I was getting some ideas. (No, no, not what you are thinking; get serious.) It was early so I suggested we go into the hotel bar for a little and relax. Elke was agreeable and we found a nice comfortable booth where we could talk. I ordered a glass of draft beer and Elke decided on white wine, now to talk.

"You know my dear", I told her, "I have enjoyed your company immensely and you have been a big help to me with your language skills. I think the time has come however, under the circumstances as they have recently developed, that we think about sending you to join your mother and the Thatchers as soon as possible. I must finish my job without your help. Once I have done what I must in Austria, likely no more than a few days with your help, I think we must get you on your way to England."

I thought the idea of being back with her mother would please her. Was *I* ever wrong! She sat there with big tears in her eyes and such a woebegone look on her face that I slid over next to her to give her a hug. When she could get some words to come out she said, "Oh, William, I don't want to go without you. I have grown so fond of you now and I hate to think you may be facing some dangers that I might help you avoid." I told her I really appreciated her concern but I was mostly worried about *her* safety. I could likely function more efficiently if I was no always afraid some of Bruno's henchmen might track her down. She looked so much like my dear Grethel I said, that if anything *were* to happen to her I would be absolutely devasted. She finally said perhaps I was right and it was for the best, we finished out drinks and went up to our room. We must leave pretty soon to meet with Roberta and her friend.

I told Elke I had brought some pictures of Grethel and I wanted her to see how much she resembled her. I hadn't looked at them myself since the time I brought them out for Major and Ethel Thatcher to see. As we sat looking at them, I realized with a shock that actually Elke looked enough like Grethel to be her twin; at least it seemed so to me. Elke took one of the larger photos, went over to the mirror, and held it beside her face to study both of them. I stood behind her and the ideas I had been pondering during our walk now seemed even more likely.

As we stood there looking at the reflections, I Asked Elke if it would be much of a problem for her to arrange her hair in the same style as that of Grethel's in the photo. She said not at all really and proceeded in a few minutes to fix her hair exactly as Grethel was wearing hers. It was amazing; now I would defy you to tell me, which was which. I told her then what I had in mind.

CHAPTER ELEVEN

ROBERTA AND HER, FRIEND, "Bob" met us at the front of the hotel, where we had been waiting, at seven-thirty, sharp. Bob then drove us down to a nice restaurant on the river. We had a window table with a view of the river. Across the river was Hradcany Castle. It was dark by now so the castle was illuminated. What a spectacular view! I thanked Bob for bringing us to such a nice place for dinner, which, he had informed us, was on him and Roberta. We had a delicious meal complete with appropriate wines. As we sipped on our coffee, I brought out the wedding pictures, which I passed to them to examine. Now was the time to tell my plan.

First, I waited for them to have time to look at the photos, which they now passed back and forth between them. Soon I saw they were looking from the photos they held of Grethel and then at Elke. Finally, Roberta asked, "Tell me Deputy, is this Elke that you have with you or is it your wife, Grethel?" Bob said, "Yes, I can't really tell them apart." I told them that was what I was waiting to hear.

Now, if they could get me a US passport for Elke with Grethel's name and photos of Elke as she looked now, I think we could have an even to good chance of getting over the border and into Austria without Elke being spotted. There, with Elke's language skills, I should soon find out what information there was, if any, about what had happened to Evan Evans. I will also seek any additional information there might be on the network we were investigating. That shouldn't take more than a few days. We will then make our way to Switzerland to check on the bank account numbers Grethel had given me.

Before I check with the bank, I will get Elke on the first flight available to England. She will wait there, with her mother and the Thatchers, for me to finish my investigation. Elke of course protested she should remain with me until I also could leave for England. Finally, the three of us convinced her however, that if we could get her as far as Switzerland without being identified, we would indeed be very lucky.

We agreed then that Roberta would pick up Elke at the hotel at nine o'clock tomorrow and they would have photos taken. I will meet them for lunch at the same café where had eaten the first time we met Roberta to compare notes. Bob said he thought he could have a passport ready by that evening. If all goes as planned, we will leave the next morning for Salzburg. We will meet for dinner and make our final plans. I told Bob I hoped he knew of another good restaurant and this time the evening was on me.

As we walked to where we had left the car, I lagged behind to talk with Bob. When I was sure Elke couldn't hear, I asked Bob if he could get me a Kevlar vest. One of those had saved my life the last time I had any dealings with these people of the escape network and I was going to be a little nervous to go on without one. I didn't want Elke to know anything about it. If somehow my wife found out about it, I knew she would worry herself sick. I didn't want that to happen; especially now that she was pregnant. Bob said OK, he would check out getting a vest for me and let me know. Bob and Roberta dropped us off at the hotel and Roberta reminded Elke she would be picking her up at nine, in the morning in front of the hotel.

The next morning, after Elke had fixed her hair as the photo showed Grethel's, we went down to wait in front of the hotel for Roberta to arrive. This will be the first time that Elke will be away from me since I found her and her mother in Berlin. It doesn't seem possible that two weeks have already gone by. I guess I was just a little nervous now not going to with her should there be an emergency but I think we are still safe here. Roberta seems very capable in any event. As I handed her into Roberta's car I told them both I would see them at lunch as we had agreed.

I went back up to the hotel room and phoned Bob. He told me he would have the vest later today and I asked if he could also get me a shoulder holster for the Glock. I wanted to wear it under my jacket. If I had a need for it, I surely won't have time to search for it among my luggage. Right now, I don't think there is a need for it but by the time we get into Austria or maybe Switzerland, things might change. The longer we are here the more time for our network friends to track us down. I suspect they may have people all over this part of the world they can call on to help look for us. I hope to have Elke on her way before that happens. That should further confuse anyone looking then for a couple.

Bob said he thought I was right; incidentally, he had all he needed for the passport in the name of Grethel E Thomas. He was just awaiting the photographs. We agreed to make the exchange of everything that night at dinner. I said this time dinner was on me. I hoped he knew another really good restaurant for us and he promised that he did. We agreed that he and Roberta would pick us up at seven-thirty. It was now the time for me to meet the ladies at the café to see how things went and take Elke back to the hotel. We will walk, giving us one last chance to see the sights of this interesting city.

Chapter Twelve

EVERYTHING WENT AS WE had planned. After the ladies had made their obligatory visit to the ladies room to repair makeup, Bob and I decided a similar trip was needed. When we returned to our table, I was wearing the vest under my shirt and had the holster for the pistol on under my coat, sans Glock for now. After we were all seated again, Bob gave Elke her new passport. He said then, for the rest of the night, we would only address her as Grethel. That is the only name she should *ever* use until all this was over. To do otherwise could well prove to be a fatal error. Everyone agreed, this was the only prudent thing to do. I suspect that if the real Grethel knew what was going on *she* would be somewhat less than thrilled.

We had an outstanding meal! We made it a memorable one, really. I thanked Roberta and Bob for all they had done for us. In the short time we had been in Prague, we had become good friends. I gave each of them one of my Deputy Sheriff business cards and put my Email address on the back. For now Grethel and I, the real Grethel, were in a rental I told them but they could always reach me through the Sheriff's office or my Email. If they were ever in California and did not visit, I would be very unhappy with them. They assured me they would accept my invitation. They were not married of course and might never be on the same assignment again but they were rotated back to the US periodically and we would likely see them individually. In any event, they would contact me beforehand by my Email address. They would be the Prague Roberta or the Prague Bob. When we met in California, we would find out who they really were.

Chapter Thirteen

W<small>E HAD AN EARLY</small> breakfast and as I had requested, our Audi was out in front of the hotel waiting for us, washed, gassed and ready to go. I figured we would cross the border somewhere south of Cesky Krumlov. If I was reading the map correctly, we have about 150 miles to the Austrian border. The route I intend to take more or less follows the Vltava. It is not a high-speed road so I figure we will need about four hours or so to reach that point. We would find lunch and top off the gas tank, somewhere near Cesky Krumlov. That was supposed to be a very interesting and ancient city with its origins in olden times. If we have the time maybe we can spend a little time exploring before we cross into Austria.

Once we got away from the outskirts of Prague, the scenery became increasingly more interesting. As we proceeded south, the mountains were getting taller and the countryside more wooded. I guess this must be a part of the Bohemian Forest. It would be nice to explore a little if we had more time.

It was nearing eleven when we reached Cesky Budejovice. It was so interesting we just had to look around a little. There was so much medieval architecture. The medieval part of the town actually dated back to the twelve hundreds although there were Romans settled here from around the time of Christ. This was truly an ancient land with people living here during the Bronze Age and before. This city, we discovered, has one of the largest arcaded town squares in all of Europe. In the eighteen hundreds, a horse-drawn tramline ran from here to Linz in Austria. And, believe it or not, this is the original home of Budweiser Beer; named after the city. Brewing is still a major industry. What an interesting place!

It was only about another hour to Cesky Krumlov and although there was much to see there as well, we had spent too much time in the home of Budweiser for more than just a few minutes looking around. On the outskirts of town, we found an attractive café where we could get a beer and sandwich. We gassed the car then and headed the few remaining miles to the border. We both were a little nervous wondering how the new passport was going to work. Maybe we will be lucky and have the same reaction as the last time we had a border crossing.

It was exactly one o'clock when we drew up to the guard post and were waved on by the Czech guards. We then drove the few remaining yards to where the Austrian Border Guards were waiting. The moment of truth was upon us! There was a guard on each side and I hit the window button and courteously rolled down the windows. The guard gave me the usual, "Passports, bitte;" and I handed over our two passports. The one on Elke's side asked, "Sprechen zie Deutch?" She answered in English that she had studied the language in school and she thought she spoke it fairly well. They continued then in German and they were talking too fast for me to understand more than a word or two occasionally. By now, the passports had been passed to the guard questioning Elke.

I asked the guard on my side if he spoke English and he answered, "Nien." I guessed I wouldn't have very much to say. I told Grethel I could not understand a word being said and she said she would explain later. Her guard had just asked her if we had been married long. I suggested that if she still had some of the wedding pictures in her purse they might want to see them. I could tell from her tone of voice that was just what she had done and then both guards were at her window. She had some of the pictures out then and they were looking at them very carefully. There were some from Las Vegas and some from Disneyland. We had thought this might happen and I had briefed Elke a little on both places so she could answer some questions.

Fortunately, all the pictures had the dates they were taken on them. The guards seemed mostly interested in those from Las Vegas and Disneyland. Grethel seemed to be fielding their questions without any trouble. I had told her not to make up any answers. If she did not know an answer, she only need say that she didn't know, she had only been one time and would know more after she had a chance to go again. It was always possible the guards could know a little about both places as they both were constantly being written up in European newspapers and magazines. Finally, they both smiled; the guard returned to my side. He handed me the passports and said, "Welcome to Austria, Herr Thomas, we hope you enjoy the rest of your honeymoon. The gate was then raised and I drove slowly through, headed for the city of Linz.

Neither of us said a word for a while; then I asked Grethel to be on the lookout for a place for us to stop and get a glass of beer. I think I needed to calm my nerves just a little right then. We had reached the outskirts of Linz by then which is only about thirty miles from the border. We found a place almost at once that appeared quite pleasant and with tables outside. There was parking just adjacent and we pulled in and found a place at one of the tables. We had a waiter at our table almost at once. Grethel said she would split a sandwich with me and I ordered one with glasses of what turned out to be very tasty draft beer.

I said it looked to me like the border guards had been looking for Elke. It is well we had planned for such an eventuality and had Grethel carry some wedding pictures in her purse. Anyway, it seemed to have worked as we had planned. Obviously, both guards did understand some English. It is a good thing we had also previously decided we would assume as much even if we wer told otherwise. It looks like we did everything right so far. I have a sneaking suspicion however; we may not have had the last of people checking on us. If they had pictures of Elke, which seems likely, the likeness is going to be obvious. She will continue with her hair fixed in Grethel's style and try to keep her makeup similar.

I didn't want to hang around Linz. This is where good old Adolph and a couple other unsavory characters from his regime were from. One of the extermination camps was just twelve miles east. I didn't think we needed to visit that either. It is only about eighty miles to Salt City by way of Wels and Vocklaburg. Wels was originally a Roman city named Ovilava and it was the capital of the Roman Province of Noricum. Those old Romans sure did get around, didn't they? Oh, Salt City?--- Salzburg, of course.

We followed the same procedure as in Prague and got direction ns to the Tourist Bureau. The lady that waited on us spoke English and I explained to her that we were finishing our honeymoon with a tour of Europe. From here, we would go on to Switzerland and then Paris before going back to California by way of London. Likely, we would only spend a day here before resuming our journey. She told us she assumed we knew this was the birthplace of Wolfgang Amadeus Mozart. No doubt, we would wish to see his home and the other exhibits relating to his life and music. I assured her that was one of the reasons we had included this city in our itinerary. She then phoned and made hotel reservations for us. She assured us it was a very nice hotel and gave me directions on how to reach it.

It was very nice all right. I'm glad now I have a little help with my expenses. We were met at the entrance by attendants who took our luggage and car keys. They ushered us into the hostelry and seated us at a small desk in order to register and present our passports. No standing at a counter for the likes of us, thank you. The room was the equal of the one we had in Prague although not as good a view. Also----no bucket of iced champagne. I hope they don't expect that we will tell our friends about *this* place! Sheesh, and at these prices?

Well it is still early evening so I think I should give the local "Bob" a jingle. I think I will just try out that cell phone this time. If there *is* anyone still checking on us, I do not want a mysterious call to show on the hotels list of calls from our room. Well, I guess it works. The call was answered on the first ring and "Bob" came on moments later. I told him I was on the cell phone, gave him its number and also the hotel name and our room number. He said we should meet. He gave me the name of a restaurant that was near to our hotel and said we should be there at seven. I agreed that we would be there. He said he knew what we looked like and would find us. "Tell the Maitre D, when you get there that you are expecting friends and get a booth for four. And, by the way, welcome to Austria, Deputy. 'Glad you haven't had to shoot anyone yet." He chuckled as he hung up.

Chapter Fourteen

WE HAD BARELY BEEN seated, when a friendly appearing couple was led to our table. "Ah, how delightful to meet our friends Herr and Frau Thomas from California," the man said. I stood then, clapped our friend on the back and as we shook hands and told him, "Bob, what a pleasant surprise. We are so happy you could join Grethel and me." All this conversation carried on of course in loud jovial voices. When we were all seated, we resumed talking but in voices that did not carry beyond our booth. Bob told us the lady with him was "Jane", which we knew of course was not her real name. We assumed she was also an agent. Bob said he had some not so good news but first let us order a magnum of champagne. We need all the appearance of a festive gathering of old friends.

The champagne was brought, along with the appropriate tableside ice bucket. When the sommelier had ceremoniously opened the bottle and poured for us, he bowed, said for us to enjoy or wine and left us. As we took sips of our champagne, Bob suggested we order diner, then we would talk. When the first course had been set before us, Jane began by telling us that they thought that it was now generally believed that I was indeed travelling with my wife, Grethel. That was the *good* news.

The *not* so good news was that they believed I had now been identified as the one who had first discovered the escape network that was now being so thoroughly investigated. There were still a number of those people about who had good reason to believe punishment for their past crimes was imminent. Many were expecting to use that network to change identities and get out of Europe. At least some of these people now knew I was personally responsible for a few of their number "*taking an early retirement.*" These people now also believed that because of my interference, it was now going to be more difficult to use that escape network. In other words, with the people here still hoping to rely on the network, I was now definitely, persona non grata to say the very least. Well, isn't that encouraging news?

I told Grethel/Elke then I was sorry if I had now put her in danger. She said I was not to be concerned. Living under the thumb of the Communists for so long had accustomed her to living with a certain amount of danger as part of her daily life. She was satisfied that I would do my best to keep her from any harm. If that didn't work out then, so be it. Regardless, we would just continue trying to do our best. I told her then that she was so like Grethel that it was uncanny. It must be something in their genes, I surmised. Jane then told us that, although *we* knew the assumption to be false, many others believed that Grethel had been privy to all that her father had been doing with the network. Likely Elke, who was now Grethel, was in as much danger as was I. I wonder how much more of this good news we can stand?

Now Bob took over. We had started our main course by then and I must confess, things seemed to have lost much of their flavor. Since they had been in touch with Al Clarke, some time ago, he said, they had known my original purpose in coming to Europe had been to try to find out what had happened to Grethel's father or possibly even locate him. They had been working on this for over a week now to help me out. They owed me for all I had been doing for them. The information they had been able to gather did not contain any good news.

It appears that the Stasi who had picked up Grethel's father were some of those same people working for or hoping to use, the network. Apparently, those running the network had decided that Evan Evans was not to be trusted and was a danger to their operations. The Stasi had all the tricks of the KGB as well as some nice ones of their own. It appears Herr Evans likely died within hours of being taken from the Austrian prison. The network was still anxious then to know what information he had. By now, they knew that most of the free countries of Europe were planning to prosecute those accused of war crimes and crimes against humanity. It was quite likely Evans by now could have been prepared for this eventuality and had a cyanide capsule. He was surely well aware of the reputation of these people by then.

Not wanting to risk being discovered with the corpse of a British subject in their possession, his captors decided on his immediate cremation. That was quickly done; the ashes were scattered on the Danube east of Linz, appropriately, near the former Nazi death camp.

Much of this information that they had uncovered was from a lower level former Stasi, promised immunity for his cooperation. Bob was certain the information they had gotten was legitimate. I thanked him and said I would give this information to Grethel when I returned home. I suspect this is what she had feared as she had firsthand experience with these people.

Bob said that, if we were agreeable, this is what they had planned: Undoubtedly, we remembered the couple we had traded places with at the airport in Berlin. Tonight we would again change places with them. We would look much as we did when we traded places at the airport. This time however there would be no rush. He gave me their room number, the same as ours, amazing. He gave us the new room number we were now to occupy where some old friends were going to gather to have a little party. You know, old friends meeting in a foreign country. The party was at nine PM. We would be there.

Well, it was interesting. We had only seen each other about three minutes at our first meeting. As soon as we had arrived, our hosts had called room service and ordered a platter of assorted hors d'ouvres and a magnum of champagne. My gosh, we will have champagne coming out our ears soon. The food and wine arrived soon and we settled down to chat. They didn't tell us their names of course but before .long we felt we were indeed old friends despite the short time we had been together.

An hour passed and I exchanged the keys of our Audi for the keys of the Ford our substitutes had been using. They had flown directly to Prague after their stint in Berlin and had been waiting for any further assignment. They had left there before us but had not tarried to sightsee along the way as we had. While we had been having dinner with Bob and "Jane", they had switched luggage; transferring our things into their bags and ours to theirs. They had finished all this just a half hour ago, working like beavers. They thought they had earned the champagne and hors d'ouvres and we agreed. We shook hands as we left and I said I hoped we would someday see them again.

Herr und Frau Thomas will be checking out tomorrow morning, heading for Switzerland. They had passports that duplicated ours. They had handed us our substitute passports as we parted. We would leave in the afternoon for Innsbruck by way of Bad Ischl. Somewhat of a roundabout way but we were killing time and would be sightseeing. We planned on a day in Innsbruck and then would go on to Switzerland.

As we prepared to call it a night, Elke told me she was disappointed to find that our substitutes had two beds in their room. She was hoping for just one that we must share. She sure knows how to scare me and delights in my expressions of dismay. I should know better by now and not let her get to me. I wonder what she would actually do if, when she said something like that, if I were to jump into her bed. I will never try to find out, believe me. Well, it has been a long day and I know we are both now ready to call it a night. I barely remember getting into bed. Have I recently mentioned to you that clear conscience thing?

Well, it is now time for us to start our new lives. Last night Elke and "Grethel" had experimented so they could have hairstyles as nearly like their substitute's as possible. The substitute Grethel even took a couple of the wedding pictures for her purse. We were careful to choose some that showed Grethel at a little distance. Hopefully, they might again be helpful. They had turned out to be so for as, for sure.

Everyone seemed to accept us as John and Hazel McDonald of Keokuk, Iowa when we went down for breakfast. Our passports, as we had been told, showed we had been in London, Berlin and Prague before arriving here. I sure hope nobody asks me anything about Keokuk, I've never been there in my life. As soon as we finished breakfast, I notified the desk we would be leaving shortly. I asked them to please make a reservation for us at a nice inn or pension in Bad Ischl and was assured it would be taken care of. They would have the information on that when we checked out. Phone the desk when we were ready and a man would come for our luggage. I handed over the keys to the ford and asked that it be brought around to the front for us. As we went up to get our luggage ready, I cautioned Elke, Hazel, that she only knew a few words of German that she had picked up in a phrase book. She understood. We have been speaking English so much lately she sounded more and more like an American and that pleases her.

Actually, it is not much more than an hour's drive to Bad Ischl so we did not get underway until elevenish. It really was a pretty drive. This is alpine country with woods, streams and lakes in profusion. I suggested to Hazel/Elke, that perhaps I should yodel; this seemed like the perfect setting. I was informed that likely the echoes would be much better later in the day, much later. Apparently, the news that I have the singing voice like that of the proverbial thrush has not yet reached this Far East; unfortunate. We spotted a cute café by one o the thirty or so lakes that are around Bad Ischl and stopped for lunch. We have a little time to kill and to sightsee before we make our way to our reserved accommodations. Too bad that we couldn't do a little fishing; it looked like the perfect place for it.

Our accommodations we discovered were at a most attractive inn. It was in the typical Tyrolean style with steep pitched roof, half-timbered walls and flower boxes under the windows. All surrounded by handsome trees, shrubs and flowers. We had decided to rest a bit before touring the town and having that exceptionally clear conscience, of which by now you should be painfully cognizant, I dropped off asleep at once. I had whispered to the lady that checked us in that I snored quite badly and we had two beds. Elke, strangely, made no comment on this when we were shown to our room. I hope she is not coming down with something.

Ischl, as the locals call it, is quite interesting. The first *written* records of the town date back to 1262. Salt has however been mined here as far back as the Iron Age and some salt production is still carried our here and also in some of the nearby towns. We were told there was a salt plant we could view but I didn't think watching saltwater evaporate would be all that exciting; maybe on our next visit. Tourism is the main business here and it is easy to understand why. With the interesting medieval architecture and beautiful alpine scenery, it is a wonderful place to visit. Elke is having a great time.

Francis Joseph, Emperor of Austria and Kind of Hungary had his summer residence here. His villa was open to the public and the first place we visited. Aah, my kind of place. I know somewhere along the line a terrible mistake was made. I know I should have been one of the royalty living right here or in a place just like it. What in the world could have happened? Franz Lehar and Johannes Brahms also spent time in Ischl. The Lehar home was also open to visitors and we toured that as well.

Our accommodations also entitled us the use of the spa facilities so we did some ritual soaking in the various therapeutic pools before getting ready to go to dinner. Our Concierge had recommended what he said was a very nice restaurant on the banks of the River Traun. At our request, he had made a reservation there for seven o'clock. I had also asked that he make a hotel reservation for us for tomorrow in Innsbruck, if possible, at the Grauerbar hotel. I had stayed there right at the end of the war for a few days and it would be interesting to see if it had changed very much. We had a delightful dinner. It was interesting watching how Elke had been changing day by day. I guess the freedom from stress and worry, now that she was away from Berlin and Bruno and his kind, was making a different person of her. We have become good friends in the weeks we have been together.

We started out for Innsbruck after breakfast. It is really not very far, so we will take our time and will explore any interesting sights we come across. It had turned out to be another great day for sightseeing so it was after noon when we finally checked in at the hotel. The Grauerbar did not look vastly different than I remembered although obviously, some refurbishing had been done. It appeared more was to be underway soon. Innsbruck is a very popular tourist Mecca and the hotel is beginning to reflect the prosperity tourism has brought to all of the Tyrol after the war. I didn't mention my previous visit. I doubt anyone would have been too impressed to learn a lowly American Lieutenant had once occupied one of the small rooms at the back of the hotel. I do remember now though, the beds then had down mattresses and comforters.

As soon as we had gotten situated in our room and had a chance to freshen up a bit, I got out the cell phone and gave the local Bob a call at the number I had for this city. As usual, it was answered at once. When I had given our location, I was told a car would pick us up in fifteen minutes. Be out in front of the hotel. With that, he rang off. Well that was short and sweet. I explained to Elke and as were all ready anyway we went down to the lobby. We had barely stepped through the front doors when a car drew up in front of us. There were two men in the front. One got out, opened the rear door and said, "Welcome to Innsbruck, Deputy; both of you please get in. We pulled away immediately. Oh, oh, I think I smell trouble.

I asked, OK, what's up, Bob? He told me would talk in just a few minutes. Let's save it all until then. We drove for a few minutes into the old part of the city and stopped in front of what appeared to be a very nice restaurant. We sat there, waiting. Before long, another car pulled up and parked behind us. A man and woman got out and hurried inside. I thought they looked a little familiar but they went by so quickly I couldn't be sure. We sat there a few minutes more. It was obvious the two in the front seat were now carefully looking up and down the street. At last, they nodded to each other, the local Bob said we might as well go in. He got out, opened the rear door for Elke and me and we all quickly went inside.

In addition to the main dining room, the restaurant had a number of side alcoves, almost little rooms, that had a heavy drape that could be drawn across their entrance. We went into one of these. There were three people already there. The two people that I had thought looked familiar were Prague Bob and Prague Roberta. The third person was a bigger surprise, it was Berlin Bob and he looked like he was tired. There must be something really important afoot. He asked us all to sit down; there would soon be a simple lunch and beer brought in. Turning to Elke he said, "I am sorry we had to meet again under these circumstances but there have been developments that need all our attention." He handed her a copy of the local newspaper and asked her to translate an article in it for me.

It seems that an American couple had been involved in an auto accident the day before yesterday. It had happened on a mountain road just outside Kitzbuhel. Apparently, a tire had blown while they were travelling at a high rate of speed and the car had left the road, crashed in a shallow ravine and burst into flame. It was believed they had been killed instantly. Identification recovered by the police indicated they were a couple from California that had been here on their honeymoon. Embassy official had taken charge of the remains for transport to the US. I looked at Berlin Bob questioningly.

He told me that yes, of course they had investigated; it had been no accident. They had recovered what was left of the device that had been used to blow the tire. Obviously, it had been radio controlled. They believed that the victims had been pursued and forced to speed up and the tire then blown, probably on a curve. They wouldn't have had a chance. I guess those people must believe I was still involved in the efforts to smash their organization. Those two poor people had died because they had been mistakenly believed to be Grethel and me. I am glad she is so far away from here!

I had told Grethel this was just going to be a simple undertaking lasting only a few days. How am I going to keep all this from her? If she is tol now that I have died and worse, while on a honeymoon with another woman, I don't know what she would do. Jiminy Christmas! Now what am I going to do? What am I going to do with Elke? I guess I was just a damn fool to have ever left California. All these thoughts were racing through my head as I digested these new developments. Elke's face now was white as a sheet, I noticed, as she realized that it could easily have been us in that burning car.

I guess I had made a mistake in taking on Elke as my interpreter. I had thought I would be saving her from the untoward advances she might face in Berlin and it seems that instead, now she might be in danger of being killed. When I tried to apologize for my blunder, she told me I was not to be concerned; she would much prefer taking her chances being with me than staying in Berlin and have to deal with Bruno and the likes of him.

Berlin Bob said he knew we all realized we faced some problems. It appeared obvious that the network, whoever they were, now knew who and where I was. It also appeared likely that they believed Elke to be Grethel and in possession of information about them she had gotten from her late father. Bob said under these circumstances, it appeared the best plan was to get Elke and me out of Europe as soon as possible. I said I agreed, we must get Elke to England at once. Major Thatcher would see she was cared for until I could join them. Please telephone the Major and advise him of the situation. I will give them the number.

As for me, they can get rid of the car we had been using. For now, I think we can safely assume that our friends believe that Elke/Grethel and I died in the crash we had just read about and are no longer a problem for them. John and Hazel McDonald will check out of the Grauerbar in the morning and disappear. If they would pick us up in front of the hotel at that time, Elke can be on her way to England in the most expeditious way they can manage. I have other things to do however. If they will drop me off at the bus terminal, I would thereafter travel by public transportation. No one would be expecting me to do that. I still needed to check out the Swiss bank accounts to see what additional information I could discover about Grethel's father and possibly the network as well.

If there any "Bobs" around Zurich I said, or anywhere else in Switzerland, maybe they can give me some phone numbers. As soon as I finish up there I will make my way to England, maybe by way of Paris. We will see how things develop. Perhaps there may be some other Bobs around there as well, in case I need help; I will have my cell phone. I will wear my Kevlar vest and carry my Glock and also my hide-out that Prague Bob was kind enough to get for me. Any information I might discover on the network I will pass on as soon as possible. I asked Berlin Bob if all this sounded workable.

"I'll tell you, Deputy Thomas," he said, "If I had not talked to Al Clarke at some length about you, I would be very reluctant to have you out there on your own. The fact remains however, the ideas you have came up with so far have worked out quite well. If Elke is agreeable, we will get her out, possibly through Paris, we will see what develops. We will have to figure out what will work best. We will phone Major Thatcher and alert him when we have the details. Elke should be in England tomorrow or the next day at the latest. As Elke still has her regular passport, she should have no problems especially with the Major at the airport to vouch for her." Elke had not said anything during all this and when Bob asked her if she was agreeable to our plans she said she would do whatever William thought best. I told her she was a brave girl and got a kind of wan smile.

Berlin Bob said he would have the phone numbers for Zurich Bob when he picked us up at ten AM. I tol him I would only take one small suitcase, the rest can go with Elke to Twyford. That was it, the meeting broke up and Berlin Bob said he would take us back to the Grauerbar.

Out meeting had lasted quite a while and it was after four-thirty as we drew up to the hotel. I suggested to Bob the sun must be surely be over the yardarm somewhere. I would dearly love to buy us all a little libation of some kind in the bar as I really felt the need of something to settle my nerves a bit right about now. Bob laughed and said he thought I had just come with one more of my good ideas. We finally found a parking space for the car and made our way into the cozy bar just off the lobby, found us a nice booth and settled in. I winked at Elke and said I figured I would probably have six or eight drinks. She laughed and told Bob I always said that and then I would only have two. The pretty barmaid who had come to our booth then took our orders.

While we waited I said, "You know, Berlin Bob, I don't know why all of you Bobs and Robertas don't form a club of some sort. You surely must have enough of you to make up a good-sized membership. It would be quite easy to remember all the names, that's for sure. Just think, you could get by with only one, perhaps quite nice, name tag and just pass it around during the meetings." Bob laughed and said, "Well, I'll tell you, Bill, we do have an organization of sorts. I regret to tell you however, it is not The Loyal and Fraternal Order of Bobs. I suspect that If I were to tell you the initials you would recognize them and likely already have a good idea what they might be. I said that I suspected that that was true. He said we were the only ones who had ever known of them as Bobs. They hadn't realized when all this started out that there would wind up being so many of them. They all kind of enjoyed it now but likely would never use that means of identification again. I said maybe the next time they would use numbers instead. I said but If I may make another suggestion, just don't use the number seven maybe more than once. He laughed and said; maybe I had a good point there also.

He told us that the other Bobs were already working on the plans we had discussed at the meeting. They were even now in the process of contacting Major Thatcher and arranging transport for Elke. The train and bus schedules they are gathering for me he will give to me tomorrow. Most likely Roberta will accompany Elke, at least until she is safely on the plane to England. I said that sure would be a relief to me. I really did appreciate all that was being done to help me out. He said don't even think about it; all the information that I had uncovered had been invaluable and they owed me. He said then it was time to go; he still had things to do and would see me in the morning. As we shook hands in parting he said, "Thanks for the drink, Deputy; I guess I needed that."

Elke had been strangely silent all this time. As we had all stood in parting, she put her arms around Berlin Bob and kissed him. She said, "I don't even know the names of any of you but I am going to miss you all. We have all only known each other a few days but it seems like you have all become the family I have needed." Bob told her, "You know, Elke, we also have grown very fond of you. We will all miss having you to look at once in a while. Even the married Bobs like to be able to see such a pretty girl from time to time." I reminded him he knew how to get in touch with me in California and that I expected to see them whenever they were rotated home. I would always know how to get in touch with Elke who would want to see them again. We parted then and Elke and I went up to the room to sort our clothing. I will just take the minimum with me. By seven-thirty we had everything done we could tonight and I suggested we go and find something to eat.

Before I left this part of Europe, I thought there was really one particular meal I would like. When we got down to the lobby I approached the Concierge and told him, I had become very fond of Sauerbraten and I wondered if he knew of a restaurant nearby where we might find that on the menu. He had a broad smile on his face as he took my arm and guided us across the lobby. There by the entrance to the hotel's restaurant, was the menu for what they had today. Today was Sauerbraten day! I told Elke that certainly had to be a good omen and she agreed. I thanked the Concierge, we went in, and the Maître D found us a nice table. I had already arranged for our checking out tomorrow morning so there was nothing more to do tonight but have an enjoyable dinner together and that is just we did.

I noticed after a while that Elke had become very quite so asked her if something was troubling her. She said that actually, she was feeling guilty. She felt she was deserting me when maybe I might need her help. Not only that; she knew she was going to miss me dreadfully. We had been together all the time now for weeks. She always felt safe when she was with me and wondered how she would feel when I was no longer close by for her to rely on. I assured her that she would do just fine. She and Roberta had become friendly and Roberta would be with her at least until she was well on her was to England. I told her she was going to have a great time there meeting her Aunt and uncle and seeing her mother again. She brightened up then and agreed that she *had* missed her mother and looked forward to being with her again. I told her that no doubt I should be with them in just a few days. We agreed, the sauerbraten was good but not quite up to her mother's standards.

Well, the morning seemed to come awfully fast and it was soon going to be time for Mr. and Mrs. McDonald to leave the hotel and disappear. I phoned the desk and a bellman soon appeared and collected our luggage. I had made all the arrangements last night so checking out only took the time to sign the credit slips and collect our passports; not that these passports were going to be much good hereafter. We were out in front with our luggage just a few minutes when the Bobs arrived to pick us up. Berlin Bob got out to greet us; Roberta we could see, was the driver today. After the bellman had stowed our luggage in the trunk we pulled away from the Hotel Grauerbar and embarked on the next part of our little odyssey.

CHAPTER FIFTEEN

IN FIFTEEN MINUTES WERE in front of a small café. Berlin Bob and I got out with Bob carrying my suitcase. Elke got in the front seat with Roberta and they immediately left. Bob and I went inside and after we were seated, ordered coffee and a sweet roll. Bob said Roberta and Elke were on their way to a small airport just outside of the city. They should be there in half an hour. A "company plane" would ferry them to the Bern airport where they will catch a direct flight to Heathrow. It will not be necessary to go by way of Paris. Roberta has decided to accompany Elke all the way to Heathrow and stay with her until she is turned over to Major Thatcher. In four or five hours, it should all be done.

We had finished our coffee by then and it was time for me to go. I took Bob's hat and he put on the trench coat he had been carrying when we entered and he left the café. In a few minutes, I put on Bob's hat and now carrying the coat I had worn as we entered, picked up the suitcase and left the cafe by the rear entrance. I crossed the alley and entered the rear entrance of the bus depot. I'm on my own now. If I am reading the schedule correctly, I have twenty minutes before there is a bus leaving for Vaduz. I bought a ticket and took a seat in the waiting room. The bus should be here for boarding before long. I think it is only ninety miles or so, so the trip should not take very long. I have been watching carefully and I haven't noticed anyone that seems to have even glanced my way. I look now much the same as many of the others waiting here. Good.

I hadn't realized this ride was going to take so long. I didn't know, when I bought my ticket, this bus was a local. It stopped at every town and hamlet and some places in between to let people off and take more on. We went through rugged alpine country almost all the way to our destination. Mountain buses do not speed and I suspect that is all for the best. The mountain scenery however was really very beautiful and I wouldn't have been able to look at if I had been driving a car. It was quite enjoyable although after a while, my seat began to feel uncomfortably hard. I decided after the first hour that it was a good idea to get off and stretch my legs whenever we stopped for a few minutes.

We arrived in Vaduz in mid afternoon. I spotted a small hotel near the bus station and walked the block necessary to inspect it. It did not look too bad; not fancy but surely just about right for a traveling businessman such as I had become. They had a room available and seemed to be glad to have me as a guest. Even better, the clerk spoke passable English. It had been a tiring ride so I decided a little nap might be in order about now. Afterward I can see about finding a place for dinner. I am fairly confident by now that I needn't explain to you again the benefits of a clear conscience. I was dozing away in moments.

I awoke frisky as a kitten in catnip. It was time now to search out sustenance of some sort. I went down to the lobby to consult with the desk clerk. Nope, no concierge here---however that did not matter; the price is right. A little conversation and I had directions to a nearby restaurant where, I had been assured, one could obtain some libation in addition to dinner. I set out to see what I might find. It seems fall is a good time to travel in Europe. Nothing is crowded. There are not yet hordes of winter sports enthusiasts abroad and the air is only brisk. I had no trouble finding a seat at the restaurant. I had an enjoyable meal while perusing a magazine I had picked up a little earlier.

I had been thinking earlier, on that long bus ride; and before you ask, no, it does not always require a bus ride for me to do that. I knew that the Principality of Lichtenstein was well known as a European banking center. Their banks flourished, because of not only the stable government and economy, but also its strict secrecy laws that governed banking operations. I decided that I would call at one of the banks tomorrow morning to see what I might learn. Not feeling much like tramping around and exploring a strange city at night, I returned to my room to see what I might find on the local televisions stations of interest. Before very long, I found it gets boring watching programs when you only recognize a word here and there. By nine o'clock I had had enough and took my magazine with me to bed and waited for that, I'm sure by now, you know what, to kick in.

I did not think there was any good reason for me to leap out of bed like a startled gazelle at daybreak. I'm sure the bankers here are much the same as in the rest of the world and believe it only prudent to await a civilized hour to begin their daily toil. I got the name of the bank from the desk and after a leisurely breakfast took a taxi to the Liechtensteinische Landsbank, the National Bank of Liechtenstein. I approached a clerk on entering and stated that I did not speak German. I wished to speak to someone who could advise me on banking in Liechtenstein. Shortly I was ushered into the office of an older gentleman---OK let's face it---my age. He smiled, stood and introduced himself as Manfred Hochstetter and invited me to be seated in one of the comfortable chairs by his desk.

I thanked him and when I was seated, told him *my* name and my address in the US. I told him I had not been in his country before but I understand that it was a well-known banking center. He said that was true they did much international banking but not a great deal with American institutions. I explained that my wife when living and working in Europe had acquired several bank accounts in Swiss banks. She held these jointly with her father. We had just recently learned he had died from an accident and that had actually occurred some time ago.

My wife was now concerned that someone might have discovered these accounts and converted them to their own use. I had come to Europe to try to discover what had caused the demise of my father-in-law and to check on the status of the Swiss bank accounts. My wife is expecting our first child soon, I explained and was therefore reluctant to leave our home and her Pediatrician in California. Before I call on the Swiss bank involved, did he have any suggestions for me? My initial thought, I said had been to transfer the accounts, assuming they are still intact, to a different bank account or perhaps even a different bank. Does that sound reasonable?

He agreed that if there was a chance the account numbers had been compromised, he assumed these were numbered accounts, in that event, I should of course, transfer those funds as soon as possible. If I wished to do so, they would be happy to open an account for me to which I could wire transfer funds if it became necessary. The Swiss and Liechtenstein banks were all in the same banking system, which made transactions between the two countries quite simple. There was a fee of course for a wire transfer but he thought I would not find it exorbitant.

When I asked, Herr Hochstetter helped me to open up an account with a small balance, got me a passbook and wished me luck in my investigations. As we parted, he gave me his business card and invited me to phone him at the number shown if I should need his assistance later. I left then to search out a place for lunch and then to arrange transportation to Zurich. Examining my maps while I ate revealed that it was only about fifty miles or so, as the crow flies, to my destination. I didn't see any of those around later however that were accepting passengers so opted to continue by bus. The route that followed may be somewhat more circuitous but I still have plenty of time. Bus service between the major cities of Europe, I discovered, is quite good with frequent departures. I was on my way again in just a few minutes.

Travel by bus was really a good choice. It was a very pretty ride along the Zurichzee which is a long, very pretty lake named for the major city at its western end. I arrived in that very city by late afternoon and had a taxi take me to a hotel catering to traveling businessmen. This time of year, it is much easier to get good accommodations as vacation times are over and the season for winter sports has not started. I figured I had enough time after checking in to rest up a little before dinner. The hotel has a dining room I noted and likely, that will do. Tomorrow morning I will check out the account numbers Grethel has given me. I decided first however, I had better use my cell phone and check in with the Zurich Bob.

Well, surprise, surprise, surprise, it was Prague Roberta. I told her I thought she was in London and she said she had been and wished she had at least had time to get out of the airport. She was, however, on the next plane out and had been here since yesterday. Being short two agents now, had required some shuffling of schedules. I said if she had a car, come and pick me up and I would be very pleased to buy her some dinner. She said for an offer like that she could make it in fifteen minutes. When she found out the hotel where I was staying she suggested we eat here; their food was as good as most and better than some. I asked her to give me a half hour, I had just arrived and should remove some of the grime of travel before greeting her.

It was nice seeing Roberta again. Other than looking just a little tired, she seemed much the same. As she grabbed my arm when we met out in front of the hotel she said, "I don't know about you, Deputy, but I'm pooped! I could sure use a little pick-me-up." I agreed; that was a very good idea and we headed into the hotel bar. It was dim and quiet and we were ushered to a nice cozy booth. I told Roberts likely I would have six or eight drinks before we ate. She grinned and said that yes, yes, she knew all about my six or eight drinks. All that Elke had done on the way to Heathrow was yak about what Wilhelm said or what Wilhelm did. "Frankly," she said, laughing, "by the time we got to the airport I was sick of hearing about what Wilhelm did or said in every other sentence. I said that I thought that Elke was really a sweet girl and I hoped everything was going to work out well for her and her mother.

I asked her if she had met the Major in London and she had. He, his wife and Elke's mother were all at the airport to meet them. I, she knew, would be interested to know that hovering in the background there and seeming to be keeping a surreptitious eye on things, was a man she remembered from some time ago. She was pretty sure he had been with either MI 5 or MI 6 at that time. If he had recognized *her*, he gave no indication. She also spotted another man nearby that she thought seemed to have eye contact with him from time to time. It could be he may have been another agent. They were just in the background however and it did not seem the ladies were even aware of their presence. The Major glanced their way casually from time to time and one of them, she was sure, had nodded to him once almost imperceptibly. Roberta said she thought it likely that my uncle must still have some residual clout with the powers that be over there.

As they had agreed on the way, Elke had introduced Roberta as a friend that had kindly consented to keep her company on the plane ride to London. As soon as all the introductions were completed and they had chatted briefly, she had excused herself and told them all she must leave. She had caught the next flight and here she was just a little the worse for wear. I said I felt I was really indebted to her for all her help with Elke and she said to forget it. It was something that had to be done.

As we were having our dinner, I told her what I had planned for tomorrow morning. I had no idea how this was going to turn out but if the accounts were still intact I would transfer them to an account I had opened in Vaduz on my way to Zurich. If I discovered anything that related to the network, or whatever it was, I would see that she got that information. She said she had a better idea. She would be at the bank to morrow also and if there *was* any information, I could hand it to her then.

That is what we decided to do. I had already given her the name of the bank. I intended to be there at ten o'clock. Roberta would be nearby in front of the bank and after I entered, she would follow. When she had determined in what part of the bank I was conducting my business she would arrange to be nearby. When she saw that I was preparing to leave, she would be ahead of me. Outside I would follow her to her car and we would return to my hotel. Seemed like a simple enough plan. I took care of the dinner check and tip and escorted Roberta to her car, which she had parked a block away. By now we were both ready to make an early night of it. I know I was.

CHAPTER SIXTEEN

I GOT A QUICK breakfast of coffee and a sweet roll. I found a taxi out in front of the hotel then and it dropped me off in front of the bank at just about the agreed time. As I paid the taxi fare, I noted that Roberta was coming up the street just a half block away. As I entered the bank, she was just a few steps behind me; so far so good. I approached a clerk on entering and stated that I had just come from the US and wished to access my numbered accounts. She asked me to wait just a moment and she would find a bank officer to assist me.

In just a few minutes, I was approached by a man I assumed must be the one going to help me. He introduced himself as Herr Gutfroinde and said that perhaps I would wish to step into an office where he would be happy to assist me. I followed him, as suggested, into a small, tastefully appointed office and was duly seated in a comfortable chair. After we were both settled, I explained that I had come from California to transfer the accounts that I had the numbers for into an account I had in Vaduz at the National Bank of Liechtenstein. My wife and I had become concerned when we learned, just recently, that her father who had a joint interest in the accounts had died. We had then learned that his remains had been cremated and his ashes scattered. We would have preferred to have made other arrangements if we had known. We were concerned now that the numbers of those accounts might have been compromised. That is the reason I was there this morning.

Herr Gutfroinde said he was sorry for our loss and under the circumstances, he could certainly understand our concern. If I would give him the account numbers, he would have the accounts checked for any recent activity. I handed him the list of numbers I had gotten from Grethel. Fortunately, they were on the stationary of this bank. He asked I wait a few moments while he checked. Thanks to computers, he was back shortly. He was pleased to inform me, he said, that there had been no recent activity. He suggested that the easiest way to handle this would be by wire transfer. I told him that is exactly what Herr Hochstetter of the Vaduz bank had suggested. He said there would be transfer fees, which I could authorize be deducted at the time of transfer. He would tell me what they were when he brought the paperwork for my signature. A clerk would bring me a cup of coffee while I was waiting.

He returned shortly with the necessary documents for the wire transfer and deduction of the transfer fees. He said he had assumed that I did not wish a partial withdrawal and had prepared the documents accordingly. I told him that was indeed correct and signed the transfer documents. He said the transfer would occur almost immediately. Later today or tomorrow, I might wish to phone Herr Hochstetter to verify everything was as I wished. I thanked him and he then handed me a bank envelope. He said it had been deposited with the bank some time ago with instructions it be given it to whoever closed out the accounts.

I knew it must be from Grethel's father. It could contain information he considered important. I asked Herr Gutfroinde if it would be an imposition to obtain a bank envelope with several sheets of bank stationary inside and he agreed that would not be a problem. I suspect they likely had, from time to time, even stranger requests. In a few minutes, he handed me the envelope and I thanked him for all his help and told him I was going to tell Herr Hochstetter how well and efficiently his bank had handled my transaction. As I walked out of the bank I put the envelope from Grethel's father in my inside coat pocket. I carried the other bank envelope, now tightly sealed, in my hand. I went out the door and down onto the street.

I spotted Roberta walking down the street and followed her as we had planned. As we reached her car, I walked up to her. A man who had been behind me suddenly came right up to me then and said, "Smile and act pleased and no one will get hurt." At the same time, another man, who had been approaching from the other direction, moved right up to Roberta; he too had a big smile as he said jovially, "How nice to meet our good friends here in Zurich." Then in a lower voice, "Look pleasant and no one will get hurt. You both have guns right at your middle. Now, hand over that envelope at once." I started to argue but smiley said, "I'm not going to say it again----Now!" Looking suitably abashed, I did as he had ordered. Immediately they melted into the crowd.

I told Roberta to get in the car quickly and get us to my hotel ASAP. We made it in a few minutes and I told her to leave the car right at the entrance. As we hurried through the lobby, I stopped at the desk and told them I must check out immediately. I had just learned of a family emergency that required I leave at once. I would be right back as soon as I pecked my bag. Please have my bill ready; I would be back shortly. Roberta went up with me, I had everything packed, and we were back down in ten minutes. I signed the American Express credit card slip, collected my passport and we left the hotel. We got in the car we had left by the entrance and were on our way thirty minutes after we had left the bank.

I had not had time to explain to Roberta yet what was going on, there had not been enough time. I explained how I had substituted envelopes and our friends would soon be looking at several sheets of blank paper. "You sure do fool a lot of people, Deputy,'" she told me. "How did you know something like this was going to happen?" I told her that of course I hadn't known for sure. When I saw the letter I knew it must be from Grethel's father and it had obviously been there for some time. It occurred to me that an employee could possibly have been bribed to make a phone call if someone came to check on the accounts. I decided it was better to be safe than sorry.

The two that held us up, I speculated, were likely contract thugs. They had to be someone who was quickly available. Likely, they always operated in this area. Most likely also, they would not open the envelope but would try to deliver it as soon as possible to their employers to collect the money they had no doubt been promised. A number of people are in for a surprise when they see those sheets of blank stationary. I suspect there will soon be a number of very unhappy campers who would no doubt be thirsting for our scalps. I had been counting on that little delay to give me time to move in case they might have known what hotel I was using. "Boy, you are really something else, Deputy," Roberta exclaimed. "I wouldn't mind partnering with you any time in the future, if the need arose." I told her I really appreciated that but now I needed to find another place to stay.

Roberta said to leave that to her. We drove to the other side of the city and to a small hotel she said they used from time to time for their own people. She would go with me to sign in. My name would not appear on any register in case anyone decided to come snooping around. Checking in only took a few minutes and I suggested we go to the room to see what the envelope might hold. Roberta said she had been waiting anxiously to see what we had.

The first sheet was a letter to Grethel from her father. It said that if she was reading it she would know that he was no longer alive. He hoped she would forgive him for the foolish mistakes he had made. He was sorry if any of those things had caused her trouble in any way. He had started innocently enough just helping out a few people. Before long, the money involved became important to him and he was soon heavily involved with people he now knew to be not only criminals but also some who were very unsavory, even evil, individuals indeed. He was disgusted and ashamed of himself but could then find no way to break away. He was sure those people had become suspicious of him. He was also well aware of what he might expect of them in the event he was taken their prisoner and likely tortured. He had taken certain precautions to keep that from happening. He was pretty sure now that his days might be numbered which is why he had written this letter. He hoped the money in the accounts in this bank would be enough for her to establish a good life for herself. He wanted her to know that he had always loved her and hoped that she would not judge him too harshly. It was signed, "Your loving father." Oh my, how sad this is going to be for Grethel even though she is no doubt half way expecting it.

There were three more sheets of paper. Evan Evans had listed the names and particulars of those he could remember. He gave the names of those who had already escaped, their new names, if he knew them and where they had gone, if he knew. He then listed the names of several others, including one woman, he believed were the ones currently running the operation and what information he had on each of them. He suspected there could possibly be many more that he did not know about.

Roberta said this was great. It was something they could really put to good use. I told her the lists were hers. I would deliver the letter to Grethel later. That would be of no use to them. She agreed. She would make some copies of the remaining sheets and fax the original to Berlin Bob. She said, "Isn't this Bob business silly, Deputy? I don't know why we ever started it. Just between us at any rate, Roberta really is my name.

I told her, "It is a pleasure to know you, Roberta; I suspect it is just as well the general public does *not* know your names. The job is dangerous enough as it is."

I suggested she pick me up after she had taken care of her chores and I would take her to dinner. I had another idea I wanted to try tomorrow and would run it by her then. She said, "Deputy, the people that hang around with you lead kind of an interesting life, don't they? I will pick you up out in front about six thirty." Good that will give me a little time for a shower and to flop down on the bed for a few minutes. I think the old batteries need a little recharging.

I was out in front at six thirty and Roberta pulled up just a few minutes later. I told her to pick out a good place to eat and we took off. As we were sitting over our coffee, I brought out the piece of paper we had gotten out of Grethel's luggage. I passed it over and asked what she could make of it. I told her where we had found it, as she looked it over.

When she said she hadn't the faintest idea what it could mean, I told her Grethel's ideas. Having just been looking at the bank numbers of the accounts I had just transferred I said I had to agree they sure did appear similar. I had decided that tomorrow, I would go to the Schweitzerisher Bankverin that Grethel thought might be what those initials stood for. I understood it was one of the biggest banks in Switzerland. Who knows, if these are indeed active accounts maybe there could also be some additional information about the organization. I wondered if by any chance she would like to go along with me. She laughed and said, "Just try and stop me, Deputy."

I said that of course, we might run into the same sort of trouble we had encountered today. If so, we should be prepared. If we happen to run up against the same two we had seen earlier today, they might this time be just a tad hostile. It is quite possible they may have resented being made fools of. If they had not collected the payoff money they had undoubtedly expected, we can expect they could even be quite irate. If those same two come up against us again they might not even bother to speak at all but just take direct action at once. Did she want to take that chance? I could likely handle this on my own. She said then, "For God's sake, Deputy, don't you think it possible we may have had some little training for such situations? I will be there."

Of course, we might be worrying about nothing. The numbers

may not mean anything. If it does develop they are in fact accounts established by out late friends, Joachim and Emil, I will transfer them to Grethel's bank in California. They owe her that much, after all they and their friends have put her through. If that is how things work out, that should just about end things and I can take off for good old LAX and then, home sweet home. Let us hope for the best. I told all this to Roberta. She said it was just as well to be prepared for anything even if it did develop that we had no cause to be concerned.

I said OK then, let's do it this way. We will go to the bank together. I will introduce you as my wife, Grethel. I'll say that we have established our permanent residence in the US and we now wish to transfer all our funds in European banks to the ones we have established in the US. At this time we would also wish to take possession of any documents we may have left on file here with those funds. Then we will have to wait and see what develops. Roberta couldn't think of anything to add to that plan and, after driving me back to the hotel, said she would pick me up in front of the hotel at ten the next morning.

Before I had left California I had picked up a sheet of Bank stationary from Grethel's bank and had copied the numbers on that as well as the number of her bank account. I also had one of the bank's envelopes in which I had put this. The paper we had from the luggage was so wrinkled and smudged I doubt if any bank employee would accept it. On the bank stationery, I had also added all the information necessary for a wire transfer. I had this with me when Roberta and I walked into the bank. The bank was crowded. It was a Friday and it seemed everyone must have been trying to get their banking business out of the way before the weekend.

After we had stated our business, we were invited to have a seat in the lobby until a bank officer would be available to assist us. Thirty minutes later two men approached where we sat. The older of the two, Herr Chretien, introduced himself and then the younger man as a trainee of the bank. If we did not object, he would like the trainee to be present to become familiar with a transaction such as ours as a part of his training. What could we do? I of course said we had no objections and we were then ushered into a small office and offered coffee, which we both declined with thanks. I explained again the purpose of our visit and passed the bank envelope to Herr Chretien. He read everything carefully and then passed it to the trainee and asked he check the computers and determine the current state of the accounts.

While this was being done, Herr Chretien engaged us in small talk in the course of which I mentioned that we expected soon to be on our way back to our home in California. At that point, the trainee returned, handed him an envelope and said the accounts appeared in good order. He had instructed a clerk to prepare the necessary documents for a wire transfer as per the instructions I had provided. That envelope appeared to be the only document on file with the funds. I said I suspected that would have been all but had not been sure. He handed me the envelope, which I passed over to Roberta. I said, "Why don't you just take care of this for the time being, my dear?" She put it in the large purse she was carrying. Well, so far, so good.

As we were discussing the weather and other inconsequential subjects, a clerk appeared and passed several documents to Herr Chretien. After looking them over carefully he gave a satisfied grunt and handed them to me. He said if they appeared to be have been prepared as I instructed, would I please sign where indicated. I did that and the clerk collected them and left. Herr Chretien said we would know in a few minutes if the transfer had been completed. He suggested we wait in the office and his assistant would return shortly with that information. He must now leave us to attend other customers awaiting him. He wished to thank us for doing business with Schweitzerisher Bankverin. If they could ever help us in the future, it would be their very great pleasure.

In about a half hour, the trainee returned and told us the transfer had been sent and the Bank of America had acknowledged receipt. As we were preparing to leave, I told Roberta I was concerned now. We had been in the bank at least an hour and a half; plenty of time for someone to set something up if they wanted to do so. I didn't want to appear paranoid but I thought we should be wary. Maybe it would be best if we mailed the contents of the envelope to Berlin from the bank before we left. She agreed and we got an envelope and she arranged for the letter to go out in the bank's mail. The clerk that assisted us with that gave us directions to a nearby restaurant when we asked. We set out to locate it and did so about a block and a half from the bank. It was close to noon and we were both hungry. Neither of us had felt much like breakfast before we started out. It looked like we had been lucky so far but I wanted to sit a spell and see if anyone showed any interest in us. Roberta agreed that was a good idea.

The restaurant was crowded and we were taken to a table right in the middle of the room. For our purposes that was good. Seated across from each other, I could see all of the restaurant to the entrance. Roberts could to see all of the back of the room. I had on my vest and all my armament. I was pretty sure Roberts had something of the kind in her large purse. I told Roberta I thought I was ready now for my six or eight drinks. She laughed and agreed that sounded like a good idea; she would join me. She wouldn't want me to feel lonesome. We ordered those and took a look at the menu. Shucks, no Sauerbraten; what kind of a restaurant is this anyway? Anyway, the drinks were OK and arrived promptly. We placed our order and were assured they would ready on completion of second drink as we had asked. These Swiss are noted for their efficiency, as I am sure you are well aware.

We were enjoying our lunch. It looked like I had completed all I had come here for. I should soon be on my way to London and then home. We decided to splurge and celebrate, "mission accomplished" and order desert to have with our coffee. We had placed the order for that when I noticed two men that had just come in to the restaurant. They were sitting a table near the door. Coffee was the extent of their order and they did not seem to be paying any attention to that. They were both sitting so they could see our table and although they did not appear to be looking at us, I was pretty sure however they could see our every move. I hope they are not what I think they might be.

I was just about to mention my suspicions to Roberta when she said, "I hate to be the bearer of bad tiding, Deputy but I have been watching two men standing in the hallway that leads to the restrooms. They have been just standing there leaning on the cigarette machine for a little while now not doing much of anything. They are not looking right at us but I have the feeling anyway that they are watching us. I told her then what I had seen. Not good, if we are their quarry, they had us between them.

I told Roberta that even if our suspicions are correct I doubt they would try anything in this crowded restaurant. It was now packed with its usual lunchtime crowd. We decided to act unconcerned; to smile and appear in a pleasant conversation. We were almost four blocks from the car. It was a block and a half on the other side of the bank. That was much too far to chance it if our suspicions are correct. I told Roberta I had an idea. She chuckled and said, "You usually do, Deputy."

As we were finishing our coffee I beckoned to our waitress. She came to our table with our bill. I told her it looked like we had a problem. My wife's ex husband had appeared and brought with him some pretty bad men. I feared he meant to harm us. I slipped a fifty-dollar bill, US, into her hand with my credit card and asked if it would be possible for her to call a taxi for us as she prepared our bill and have it wait just in front of the restaurant door with car door open for us. When she knew all had been prepared she could bring the bill, I would sign and we would immediately depart. It could save the restaurant trouble as well as us. I guess the fifty got her attention. She nodded, said we could depend on her and left. It sure is a good thing so many of the people in this country speak such good English.

We chatted and smiled as we sipped our coffee for twenty minutes. Our waitress appeared with our bill and said all was in readiness. As I finished signing the credit slips, we both rose and headed for the front door. I noted Roberta had her hand inside her purse. Our waitress walked with us to the front of the restaurant which was a nice touch I had not even suggested. She stood in the door as we passed through, bade us goodbye and said she hoped we had enjoyed our meal and please come again soon.

We crossed quickly to the curb where our taxi waited with the door open. We jumped in and we were underway almost before I had the door shut. We were right; the two coffee drinkers had pushed the waitress aside and rushed outside. By then we were a hundred feet away. Their facial expressions exhibited a nice combination of rage and frustration. What a shame. Roberta said she thought the two in the back had been the two we had met the day before. The lighting had been a little too dim for her to be sure. She laughed and said she thought we had, by now, succeeded in irritating quit a few people. I handed the driver a twenty and we spent a half hour or so driving rapidly about until I figured we should have thrown off any pursuit and we were then deposited back by Roberta's car.

Before we jumped in and drove away, I suggested to Roberta we have a quick look to be sure there were not going to be any surprises. We started at the back and she took one side and I the other and worked out way forward. Anything that was done would have to be done quickly.

There were just too many people about to do otherwise. Roberta found the first one located inside the rear fender well near the gas tank. I found one inside the left front wheel well just before the firewall. It appears we must be really irritating someone.

Roberta thought they looked like little blocks of semtex; enough to give us quite a little headache if they had gone off while we were in the car. She quickly pulled out the activators and, as she suggested, I dropped them into a sewer grating a few steps down the street. Each had a tiny antenna and obviously, they could be radio activated. She would keep the explosives and send them to be analyzed. I stood outside and a little away as she put the key in the ignition. Immediately there were two little pops as she turned the key. The igniters worked all right. Sure a good thing they were not still attached to the charges. "Boy, Deputy," Roberta exclaimed. "You sure as hell saved our bacon! I should have thought of that myself. That is just plain carelessness on my part. Thanks." I said I hoped there were not any other surprises to crop up later. She suggested I get a taxi back to the hotel. She was going to turn the car in immediately and it would get a thorough going over."Thanks again, Deputy!" She would phone me sometime later.

Funny, no phone call, then the desk rang about six-thirty and told me that my wife had arrived and asked them to tell me that she would be up in twenty minutes and we had a date for dinner. Now what is going on? We know darn well it is not Grethel. Roberta must be playing a joke on me. I'm glad she phoned however, I had just finished my shower so I got dressed, prepared to go out if that is what was going to be required.

Roberta arrived at the room in due time, complete with two suitcases. She said, "Hello there, Deputy. Say hello to your new wife." I said, "Come on now, Roberta, what's up?" She said, "Well, Wilhelm, you know my dear, we really have gotten very close the last few days, don't you think it is time for me to move in with you?" When she saw the expression my face she burst out laughing. Then she told me how Elke had told her on the plane ride how she had teased me just to see the look on my face. She promised not to tease me anymore, at least for tonight. Why in the world do these women insist on doing this to me? OK, "hubby", she said then, we had a date for dinner. She grabbed my arm and we went down and strolled into the lobby. Just like an old married couple. I know, If Grethel saw this; she would kill me for sure.

I swear, if I am going to continue gathering wives at this rate I had better check in with the Mormon Church. If I find out they still allow polygamy somewhere, I may have to enlist just for self-preservation, if nothing else.

Roberta had a different car, a sleek black Fiat this time. I got in and we were on the way to our *Date*, another restaurant. To tell you the truth, I'm getting a little tired of this restaurant food. I'm ready for some good old home cooking, even if I have to do it myself. This hotel had a lighted parking lot and an attendant at the entrance. That's good. I think I will give the car just a little check before we leave anyway. Talk about your paranoia. We used the entranced off the parking lot and were shown to another small private dining room. I wasn't really surprised to see the Bobs from Berlin and Prague. There was a stranger also whom they introduced as Henri Molier. He was an Interpol agent and one of those in their department trying to unravel the workings of the network we had uncovered. First, he wanted to thank me for the work I had done so far. He was confident they would soon make great strides in rounding up those trying to use the so-called escape network and hopefully to dismantle it entirely. I thanked him and wished him every success in those endeavors. Berlin Bob then said, "Why don't we all sit down; there is much to talk about."

He started out by saying, "You are doubtless aware by now, Deputy, that you have gotten some very bad people extremely annoyed with you." The last few days, you and Roberta have made some of them look like bumbling idiots. Your tricks in getting Elke Groenwald out of Berlin didn't exactly endear you to Bruno Hauptmann either. I know you did not have time to look at the info in that last letter you shipped out to me but your friend Bruno was right there on the list the letter contained. He was apparently one of the contacts in Berlin for those wishing to use the network. Interpol put out a pick-up order on him but by the time the police went to get him, he was long gone; his apartment was empty.

Prague Bob spoke up then and said that likely very soon there was going to be a real effort to get rid of me and my wife, the former Ms. Evans, who, these people had convinced themselves, knew more about their organization than they wanted her to know. For these people I now seem to have gotten to be one great big pain in the ass. Golly, that is a real pity, isn't it.

Monsieur Molier said that for my safety I should probably get out of Europe at once. I was no doubt aware that if a professional assassin were out to get you that would happen sooner or later. Being an unpaid volunteer Deputy did not call for me to take any further risks. It would be possible to fly Roberta and me out almost immediately. I had been so skillful in switching wives around that they were sure all these people were convinced that Roberta was my wife, Grethel. He chuckled when he said that he understood I had fortunately eliminated any of those who may have actually seen her.

Berlin Bob took over then with, "However, Deputy, we may have an opportunity here. If these people can be led into making another attempt on you and Roberta, one that we orchestrate, we may be able to roll up another bunch of them as you did in California. I won't insult your intelligence by telling you there would be no risk. You certainly know better. I also k now how concerned you are about your wife learning you might again be engaged in some hazardous undertaking. There will be no hard feelings if you feel this is just something you cannot do and we will get you out as soon as we can."

Well Golly Ned! What a spot that puts me in! I know if Grethel were here she would grab me by the ear and have me out of here so fast my head would be spinning. Elaine would no doubt have a firm hold on the other ear. I also know however, if I don't help out with this I will later on always feel that I had *chickened out* when the chips were down. I'm not sure I could live with that. Obviously, I'll be dammed if I do and damned if I don't. In retrospect, I wonder what in the world led me to believe this was going to be a relatively simple matter that could be completed in just a few days; apparently another of those "senior moments". They seem to be cropping up quite often lately. Everyone was watching as I pondered all this; 'must have been a fascinating sight.

Finally, I said, "All right you guys, I'll help out------but, you must never, ever let word of this reach Grethel. I have already been gone much longer than I had estimated. I know that by now Grethel must be fit to be tied." Bob suggested I phone her and tell her I had almost wound up all the loose ends here and should be home in about a week. Likely, I will need a few days in England before heading home.

I phoned that night. It was late morning in California. Elaine answered. When she found it was me she asked, "Where in the world have you been, Bill? You weren't supposed to be gone this long." I said it was really a long story; everything seemed to be taking longer than expected. I was in good health and expected to be home in about a week. I was going to have to stop in England a couple days to see what arrangements can be made for Elke and her mother. She said Grethel had gotten a phone call from her Aunt Ethel a few weeks ago telling of my visit with them.

When I asked to speak with Grethel, she informed me she was at the doctor's office and before I got all panicky, Grethel was healthy as a horse and was just there for one of her regular check-ups. She was being very careful to see that the first of my "numerous" children was a healthy specimen. She would have to relay my message to her. She knew she was going to be upset to have missed my call. I said to tell her I would phone from England so they would know when to expect me. She might also tell Grethel I loved her dearly. Elaine said, "You know we all love you also, Bill and want you to be careful over there and please come home soon." I told her I might never leave the house again and she chuckled as she hung up.

Chapter Seventeen

WE HAD A MEETING in my hotel room the next morning. All the Bobs were there, including my newly acquired wife, Roberta, Henri from Interpol and a man from the Swiss State Police. Berlin Bob said that the latter mentioned had also been thoroughly briefed. When we were introduced he came over to shake hands, he said, and in perfect English, that he was very pleased to meet me. It was not often, he said, that one met a volunteer who had accomplished so much good. I thanked him and said it had been something I had to do. I was happy we had been successful so far. I hoped my volunteering days would be ending soon as I was anxious to get home to my family and friends, hastily adding that of course, I also considered all of those here to be my friends as well.

The purpose of the meeting was to devise a plan that would lure as many of the bad guys still hanging around here as possible into making a try to eliminate Roberta, that they think is Grethel, and me. We want to choose a place where they think their chances of finishing us off is good. So far, their batting average has not been too good and Roberta and I will be trying to insure it does not improve. The idea is to make the trap seem enticing enough that we can lure in as many as possible without putting Roberts and me in any more danger than absolutely necessary. We need something to really grab their attention. With the State police and Interpol in the team we should have a few options.

It is obvious someone had fingered us on our last visit to the bank. It seemed most likely that person must have been the trainee that had been assisting Herr Chretien. The bank manager had vouched for Herr Chretien who had been a valued employee for many years. The trainee was a new hire that had been with the bank only a short time. We are going to assume he is the one and use him to bait our trap. If we are wrong, we sure are going to be wasting a lot of time and energy for nothing

"Mrs. Thomas" and I are planning to drive to Bern to enjoy the scenery and will catch a direct flight to Heathrow from there. I will ask the hotel if they can book first class accommodations for us; probably a few days hence to give everyone time to get their act together. I will telephone Herr Chretien and make an appointment to pick up a substantial amount of cash to see us through the rest of our journey to California. He will tell us, when we come for the money, that there was an envelope that was overlooked when we last visited. He will tell that same trainee, who will again assist him, of his mistake at that time and apologize profusely to us. The man from the State Police assured us he would be discretely briefed until he could play his part. Let us hope he is a good actor. I sure hope we haven't made a mistake and it is Herr Chretien and not the trainee we should have suspected. That would really throw a monkey wrench into our plans wouldn't it? Do you think possibly both of them? Nah----couldn't be----could it?

I told Berlin Bob he should get a Kevlar vest for Roberta. I would be wearing mine for sure. I also wanted a snub nosed thirty-eight in an ankle holster for a hideout gun and one of similar caliber to wear under my belt at the small of my back. If I could think of a way to hide a machine-gun somewhere I would probably have taken one of those as well. OK; I suppose we can't have everything. I will have my nine-millimeter Glock under my left arm however. I told him this privately and said I didn't want anyone else to know about these preparations. Maybe we wouldn't need any of these things but I would rather be safe than sorry. He said not to worry; all would be taken care of. I said there was one more import detail I needed to talk over with him and Prague Bob in private.

It took three days to get everything set up. I had also conferred with the two Bobs and made certain arrangements. I sure as hell hope it all works! We decided to use Roberta's Fiat for the trip. It was a rental and we could turn it in at the airport in Bern----I hope. Our plans should be pretty well known by now by those we wanted to know them.

OK, this is the day. "The little woman," and I are heading for home. When I call Roberta that, she punches me on the arm. Naturally, I try to use it at every opportunity. The Bobs caught on soon and use it also when they can. Roberta is fit to be tied. She says if she ever got married and her husband called her that she would shoot him for sure. We arrived at the bank shortly after it opened. Just as it had been arranged, a car parked just in front of the bank pulled out just as we arrived and we took that parking place.

Herr Chretien was awaiting us. He insisted we come into his office and have coffee while we completed our business. He sat us down and poured from a carafe on his desk. I waited until I saw him take a few sips before starting on mine. I hate to be paranoid but-----. Herr Chretien summoned the trainee then and instructed him to obtain fifteen hundred pounds sterling and twenty-five hundred US dollars for Mr. Thomas and this time please do not forget his envelope. The trainee said he was sorry to have overlooked it the last time and deeply regretted any inconvenience he had caused. I told him not to be overly concerned, as it was, we had not been greatly inconvenienced. Foreign money was kept in the vault he advised us. He would return as soon as possible.

While we waited, we chatted and sipped the excellent coffee of Herr Chretien. As we were sipping and chatting, I said we had decided that, as long as it was not a great distance to Bern, we might take a detour and see more of the countryside as long as we had the time. I said that maybe we would go by way of Lucerne, then down through Interlaken and then north to Bern. It shouldn't take more than four hours and we had the time. Herr Chretien pointed out that we would start out along the Zurichzee and be near water most of the time. Lake Lucerne and the Thunzee were the biggest lakes of course but there were also many other lakes and streams all along the route we would travel. It should be a very pretty drive. He wished it were possible to accompany us. I had our roadmap open on the desk with our route marked in red and left it there.

After all that coffee, I inquired if it were possible to use the restroom facilities before we started and he had one of the secretaries go with Roberta. He showed me the location of the men's room. I hoped anyone who might be interested would have the time for a good look at the map I had left lying on the desk. You should have seen the glare I got from "The Little Woman" Well, she started all this.

CHAPTER EIGHTEEN

W ELL, WE HAVE OUR money and the bogus envelope. The Little Woman", grasped my arm and we left the bank and made for the car. As I held the door for Roberta, I told her I would lay off the little woman business if she would promise to lay off trying to get me flustered with those sexual innuendos. She said she would have to think about it. She might think of something really good to try on me before we parted company. OK, OK, if that's the way she wants to play, I won't tell her what that tiny red sticker on the driver's side window means. I put everything in gear and we were on our way to Lucerne. Maybe I will be back in Good Ole California before long.

It is just ten-thirty. We should make it to the Flughafen Bern-Belp by mid afternoon. We figure that if an attempt is going to made this morning it is probably going to happen before long. That is probably why we aren't talking much as we try to watch everything around us as we drive out of the city and south along the easterly side of the Zurichzee. I'm glad Roberta is an experienced agent. I'm sure going to need all the help I can get. The Bobs, the State Police and Interpol are all in on the act too so fortunately we are no in this on our own.

It wasn't long after we had turned west on E47, heading for the north end of Lake Lucerne, that I told Roberta to get ready. The truck that had passed us twenty minutes ago had stayed just a couple hundred yards ahead of us. The couple of times I slowed down they did also and maintained the same distance. The traffic had now thinned out considerably. This could be the time. Roberta got on the cell phone and relayed this information to our back-up.

Just as we came around a sharp curve, there was the truck; stopped! I hit the brakes and the emergency flashers shouting, NOW! Roberta dived into the ditch alongside but I had to dash across the other lane first. The rear door of the truck flew up and there were two men with automatic pistols shooting at us. They had no chance with Roberta but I had farther to go and as I was diving for the ditch one of the slugs caught me high on the shoulder and I went into that ditch head first; as if I had been shoved by a giant fist. Thank goodness the Kevlar had deflected the bullet as it had hit me only a glancing blow but I was a little disoriented for awhile. I bet anything they thought they had gotten me. As it was, it was a few minutes before I could function normally.

I could hear that Roberta had started shooting. I lay still for a few minutes until I was OK and then started moving up the ditch toward the truck. They could not see me and when I got to within fifty feet, I peeked over the edge. The driver was out of the cab now and at the back of the truck firing at Roberta also. Boy, were they in for a surprise. I got the driver with the first shot. That might keep them from driving away anyway. The men up in the back of the truck of course had automatic weapons and our pistols were no match for them. We were however close enough for them to be effective and had the ditch for cover. They also must now have one of us on either side and with nothing to hide behind. The door came slamming down after Roberta had obviously winged one of them. What did they expect to do now?

I had been wondering about our backup and here they came, sirens wailing. One had been a mile ahead and one the same distance behind. They had not wanted to spook our quarry by being too close. These were the Swiss Police part of the operation. They took over. It appeared the wounded driver would likely recover. Roberta had gotten one man in the arm. The whole episode hadn't taken more than half an hour and we were on our way again. Three more of the gang had been rounded up. I wonder if we were off the hook now. As we left, the officer in charge said they would take care of winding things up here.

We found a little café just past Lucerne and stopped for a little lunch. It was time to reload everything, catch our breath and take stock of the situation. Our only damage was a tear in the back of my shirt. Fortunately, I had been diving forward and the slug just glanced off the Kevlar and kept on going. We had cleaned off the dirt we had picked up in the ditch as best we could and on the whole, looked fairly presentable. My shoulder was getting a little stiff and sore by now and Roberta insisted when we started out again that she take over the driving or a while.

I had made a change in our itinerary from what I had suggested to Herr Chretien. Instead of going south and through Interlaken, I intended we now head straight west through Trubschachen to the airport. This is the route that I had outlined in red on the map I had conveniently left on the desk when we made or visits to the restrooms. If anyone had looked at it, they would know our actual plans. Maybe we might lure a few more into the trap before we finish the trip. I guess it might depend on just how many resources they have and just how badly they want to do us in. So far, we have been underway about two hours although it seems like it must have been much longer.

I guess we must have become pretty important. The next attempt at us came not long after we started out again. Roberta had spotted them in the rear view mirror as they got closer and closer and then at about one hundred yards just hung there keeping pace with us. I called our minders and said it looked like we had company again. We were not too far from Trubschachen when they speeded up and gave us a good hard bump. No shooting and now they had a helicopter keeping pace with us also, off to the side. They were going all out on this one. Maybe this is the A Team or part of it anyway. Obviously, they want us to speed up. I'll bet they think they can pull the same stunt that killed the two agent near Kitzbuhel. They are in for a little surprise. Even I don't know yet how big a one it will be.

Roberta is a good diver and we were cruising along about eighty when we came to a set of curves. As we screeched around the first there was an explosion. It was the car chasing us. They blew off the road, hit and tree, the gas tank ruptured and it blew up in a big fireball. We kept on going. Eventually some of our helpers will be on the scene. No big rush for that one however. Remember that tiny red sticker? It was an arrow placed on the window horizontally. It meant that our four watchers at the bank had seen the gang put the explosives on the Fiat and had removed them. The horizontal placement meant they had replaced the explosives on the car the gang members had been in. That is the secret I had worked out with the Bobs. I knew the explosives were off this car but didn't know if they were on the one that was chasing us or some other--------until now.

I hope we are getting some revenge for Bob and Jane that were blown up near Kitzbuhel. (We never did learn their names.) I hope some of those in that burning car back there are some of those that had been responsible. I suppose there could be a good chance they were. I know the deaths of those people will not bring that Bob and Jane back but sometimes revenge is just a little sweet.

I guess we are not through with these people yet. That helicopter is still out there somewhere. Right now, I can't see them. I hope they are not equipped to do anything else. We made it safely into Trubschachen. I doubt they can do anything while we are here in the city. Roberta said let's stop and get a beer and split a sandwich. Good idea. While we sat with our sandwich, I explained to her about the little red sticker. I also told her why I had not told her before. If she had just promised to leave me alone she would have known all about it. She vowed then that now she really would think of some way to get back at me before we parted for good.

We didn't waste much time In Trubschachen. We had alerted our people we were taking a breather there and called in again as we started out. We had gone ten miles or so, passed through Zaziwill and turned south onto the cut-off I wanted to take to Munsingen when all the windows blew on the driver's side. We were showered with glass. That helicopter had popped up from behind a hill and was on us before we knew it and was flying alongside us about fifty yards away. When Roberta said she was OK, I scrambled into the back seat. The windows were out and I began shooting with my Glock. I had just as good a shot at them as they did at us. Roberta was slowing and speeding suddenly, which of course they could not do. I made several hits on the helicopter and then decided to just try for the rotor. I had had good luck doing that once before. I only got off a couple shots before they saw what I was doing and immediately swung over to fly just above us.

It was almost impossible for me to get a shot off and almost as difficult for them however they did have an advantage. They got off a shot at us from time to time and I knew sooner or later they could get lucky. Roberta continued her evasive driving, swinging from side to side, speeding up dramatically and suddenly stopping. She was good and had obviously had considerable training in this kind of driving. I reached over and got out map from the front seat.

I had looked over the map very carefully when I had been planning our route. I thought I remembered something. Yes-----there it was. Might just be our best chance. I told Roberta there was a road coming up on the left very soon. As soon as she spotted it, dart into that and then give it all the gas the car will take. It's a good thing Roberta was driving. When she spotted the road, she made high speed turn, hardly slowing and dashed into the side road. The helicopter was caught by surprise and went shooting on past. We must get around that next curve before they come back and catch us. I told Roberta, GO, GO, GO! She did. We barreled around the curve with the helicopter now right on our tail. A hundred feet more and we were in the tunnel. To bad; the helicopter did not fit. We heard the crash and explosion. They had tried to pull up but there was just no room. We sure had lucked out. They sure would have got us sooner or later. We didn't see any other cars working with them so maybe now we are in the clear. Roberta pulled over to the side of the road just outside the tunnel and we both got out of the car. We were pretty keyed up after that squeaker. Neither of us had a thing to say for a few minutes.

Finally, Roberta said, "Deputy, I don't know if I want to be married to you any longer. Your wives seem to lead a life a little more exciting than I am used to. As a matter of fact, one that is more exciting than I *want* to get used to. I think I am ready to file for divorce right about now." Then she chuckled and said it sure was a good thing I had gone over the map so thoroughly or we might not be standing here joking about this now. I said, "Who's joking? I'm still scared out of my wits." Roberta said well if that was so, I sure didn't show it when we were doing our thing back there a little while age. I said I just had not realized until now that I had been scared to death. Well, that may have been," Roberta said, "and I guess I may have said this before but believe me, Deputy, when the chips are down, I'll partner with you any time. What a nice thing to say. I told her so and that I hardly thought it was deserved.

We were apparently on a secondary mountain road that was not used much. We had not seen a car or truck since we had been here. I had walked back through the tunnel but the crashed helicopter was blocking the tunnel and road. As a matter of fact it was still burning. We couldn't reach our team on the cell phone here and likely must wait until we can get some place in the clear. I told Roberta it looked like we would have to continue on this road until we could find some way to double back and perhaps get on a road to Munsingen. It took almost an hour, wandering around on little mountain roads before we were finally back on the highway. We were both a little tired by now. We could get through on the cell phone by now and explained what had happened and where they could find the helicopter. It did not appear there had been any survivors.

By now, we figured, it must only be fifteen miles or so to Belp. We will check with the team again when we reach there. At Munsingen, we head north paralleling the river until we reach the bridge the leads across and to Belp, which is just a little south of the airport a mile or so. Our reservations are for Swiss Air's four o'clock flight. Let's keep our fingers crossed. We have two hours to make it.

We were just past Konolfingen when Roberta said she thought we had another tail; a car had speeded up right behind us and was keeping pace with us. Another had come up just behind that. There were two men in each car. They were just following along behind. Well I suppose two men in a car is not all that unusual but by now I guess we had become somewhat paranoid. I got on the phone anyway and reported what we had. I was informed they would try to get us some help.

Just as we entered the next wooded area, it became obvious we were not just being paranoid. The lead car had speeded up and prepared to come along side as the other got right up on our bumper. The one on the side was a heavy sedan. I couldn't get off a shot before they rammed into our rear quarter. The other car was riding our bumper. There was no way we could withstand many more bumps from the heavy sedan or out run them. Instead, Roberta darted off the road, narrowly missing two trees and slammed on the brakes just as we were to crash into a large boulder. We jumped out of the car as our pursuers shot by on their way past us down the road. We knew they would be back soon.

We had made our way back into the woods as far as our time would allow and taken up positions where we could see and cover each other. We had tried to conceal ourselves as best we could but had only a few minutes to do so. We each had found a fallen tree for a little protection. We heard the cars return and screech to a halt out on the highway. It does not appear they intend to try to sneak up on us does it? Anyway, we sure do know they are on the way.

You could see them then working their way through the trees in two groups of two each. Not too smart; if they had spread out we could have been in some trouble trying to keep track of all of them. One gets the impression these are not exactly experienced woodsmen as they come stumbling through the trees. I had taken my stand about seventy-five feet from Roberta. When I saw them stop to listen, I snapped the branch

I was holding. I gave of a satisfying crack as I had intended and they all started toward the sound. These must be city guys; they were staying so close together.

When they got a little closer, I heaved the heavy end of the branch I was holding as far as I could off to my left. Roberta was over to my right. The branch made a satisfying crash through the branches and landed with a thump. All four of them jumped like they had been shot and two of them started shooting toward the sound. Boy, were they ever spooked. I do believe we do not have members of the A Team here. Perhaps their reserves are getting thin.

It is almost a shame to have to shoot at these guys but I guess we have no choice. They surely will shoot us if given half the chance. I picked one with his gun hand out as if he intended to shoot and tried to hit his shoulder. I had waited until they were looking the other way and they had no idea where the shot had come from. My target shrieked, dropped his gun and clutched his side. Well, close enough.

The other three obviously had no idea what to do next. I really felt a little sorry for them. Now, while they were looking elsewhere, Roberts fired off three shots in quick succession. They had no idea where those came from either. By now, the wounded man was struggling back toward the highway. The three remaining had now figured out that perhaps they would fare better if they were to separate. As they started to do that, I winged another one and when they turned toward me Roberta let loose a couple more shots and creased another of them. That did it; they quit and made their way out of the woods as best they could. We followed them as they stumbled and fell through the trees and bushes back to their cars. They all piled into one. I guess the unwounded one was the driver. The other car they abandoned. By then we were close enough to get the license number as they drove off.

Clever Roberta had grabbed the cell phone as we jumped out of the Fiat and we used that to call our team. Roberta gave them the information on the green Audi last seen heading east on the highway. She repeated the license number twice. Three of the men were wounded. They assured her they all would be picked up before they could get to a hiding place. Roberta told them that now we were without transportation as the Fiat was no longer driveable and gave them our location, about a mile and a half west of Konolfingen. OK, stay put about twenty-five minutes they told her. The next helicopter we heard should be friendly so don't shoot at it right away. Step out into the highway when we heard it and we would be picked up. We got our stuff out of the somewhat wrinkled Fiat and stood there on the edge of the woods.

It sure was quiet and peaceful now until------------------"Don't make any sudden moves Mr. Fancy Pants Deputy or you wife gets a bullet right now in her pretty little brain. You think you are so clever and you are so smart but now you are not the so smart one after all, Yah? Oh, oh, there stood a man partly behind Roberta with a pistol right at her ear. Roberta had her hands up and he reached around, plucked out her gun, and let it drop to the ground. I guess we should have checked that other car. Maybe this was the "brains" of this group. "Now Mr. Fancy Deputy," he continued, you are going to pretend to be a fancy little toad for me. Hold your little pistol between your thumb and forefinger. Now squat down my little toad and then you can toss your little pistol this way.

As I squatted down to do his bidding, then, as he said, "And now Goodbye, Mr. Fan-----" I shot him with my hideout gun just as he lifted the pistol from Roberta's ear to aim at me. Nice of him to make it a little easier for me wasn't it. "Geez, Deputy," Roberta gasped, "What are you trying to do to me. That was right by my ear!" I said, "Sorry. Roberta, with all that camo stuff on, I was afraid he might also be wearing body armor of some kind. I didn't want to take a chance. Sorry I had to place the shot so close." She picked up her gun and we went over to see our latest would-be assassin. He was unconscious but obviously not dead. He must really have one hard head. Of course, no I.D. of any kind and yep, he was wearing armor.

We had no sooner finished checking the man out than we heard a helicopter. Do you suppose this one is really ours? By now, we were both really ultra paranoid. We quickly reloaded everything. As the chopper came within sight, Roberta stepped out on the edge road but I stayed back in the tree line ready to start shooting. As soon as the helicopter started its landing, Roberta darted back into the tree line also, not far from me. We were ready.

They landed and the door opened. Now there stood one of the best sights we had seen for what seemed like years, it was Berlin Bob. Even then, we waited to see who that was behind him. It was a smiling Henri Molier. We grabbed our bags, raced over and threw them on board and then both of us were hoisted up. When we pointed out our latest assailant Bob and Henri jumped down hoisted him on board and we were away. We were both still holding our pistols. We almost could not believe this was not just one more last try to get us.

Bob smiled at little when he looked at us and said he thought we really could put up the guns now. He would take care of them for us. We were going directly to the airport. We would be in time for our flight. Prague Bob would meet us at Swiss Air with our tickets and boarding passes. He was flying with us to London------just in case.

Chapter Nineteen

It almost seemed too easy; everything really had been taken care of. We were whisked through the boarding area, onto the plane, and to our seats fifteen minutes after the landing of the helicopter, unbelievable. What a day this has been! Prague Bob sat across the aisle from me in the first class section. Roberta was next to me in the window seat. There were only four other singles riding first class, pretty much spread out. Bob told us not to worry they were all OK. Five minutes later, we were airborne. I told Bob this was a god time to catch forty winks, after which, I would likely have six or eight drinks. I heard Roberta say, "I'm with you, Deputy", just as I dropped off.

I had just barely closed my eyes when Bob was poking me. Now what? I got panicky as I reached for the Glock that wasn't there. Bob said, "Take it easy, Deputy, I just wanted to tell you that if you still want those six or eight drinks you better order pretty soon. We are going to land in less than an hour." Roberta had her head on my shoulder, fast asleep. When I nudged her, her eyes flew open. I said, "Gee whiz, Roberta, I didn't realize that just a little excitement would tire you so. If you want that drink, we had better order as we land pretty soon." "For crying out loud, Deputy, why did you let me sleep so long", she demanded. I told her, that her snoring was so interesting I had not wanted to interrupt her performance. Bob laughed and said the snoring of *both* of us was so loud the pilot had come back to check to see if there was mechanical problem needing attention. The cabin attendant took our orders and we had our drinks moments later.

As we sipped our drinks, Bob said, "You are both to be congratulated. Our plans worked out even better than we had hoped. We haven't completed the count for sure but it appears you and Roberts have accounted of at least twelve or thirteen. One hell of a day's work! There will likely be a bunch to be rounded up when the interrogations of the ones we have caught are completed. You both sure do deserve those drinks and incidentally, William, my name really is Bob. I am the only real Bob in the whole bunch. I am rotating back to DC in a few weeks so I guess it is OK to tell you. And also, incidentally, I think you are one hell of a Deputy." He put out his hand and I shook it. I was speechless.

Roberta said that was her sentiment exactly and then she gave me a great big kiss. Of course then I was blushing like some teenage schoolboy and they both then had a good laugh. I wonder if I am ever going to grow up. Bob said he had some good news for Roberta; she had thirty days R&R as soon as she got back to the states. Was she happy! This was the first time she had off in more than a year she said. As we were chatting, Bob told us to be prepared for an exhaustive de-briefing tomorrow. Likely, it could last all morning and possibly even longer. The attendant came to collect our glasses then and we prepared for landing.

As soon as everyone else had left the plane, we took our departure also. Bob had said he thought there would be a car come for us and sure enough, as we started down the stairs a big limousine pulled up in front of us. A man got out of the front and opened the rear door for us. He said for the three of us to please get in; we would be taken to our hotel. Mr. Thomas's relatives had already been notified of his arrival and that he would contact them tomorrow after his de-briefing. Off we went and before long wound up in front of a small, elegant hotel that really looked more like a private residence.

No need to register; that had all been taken care of. We were shown to a suite of rooms. Not opulent but very comfortably furnished. We were told then that we could order whatever we wished from room service when we ready. Roberta and I had not had much to eat today and thought we would do that now. Once we finished I was going to grab a good hot shower and hope I didn't fall asleep before I made it to the bed. Roberta said that sounded pretty much what she planned also. Bob said he had had a pretty busy day also and I said I sure can sure believe that. He and Berlin Bob must have been busy as birddogs in a cornfield trying to keep track of us and everyone else and getting support teams to the right places. I told him how much we appreciated all they had done to keep us alive.

We decided then, what the heck, we would just go ahead and order a good dinner, complete with champagne. We all decided that this had to be the perfect time to have just a little celebration. As we chatted over dinner, I suggested to Roberta that as long as she was going to have some time, why not come to California and visit us. She could meet the Grethel she had heard so much about. She said, maybe she would just do that. She had been so engrossed in being Grethel lately that now she felt she must see her to talk to and see what she was really like. I also reminded Bob I was expecting to see him in California whenever he could make it. He said I could count on that but he did not know exactly when that might be. By now, the three of us were pretty much ready to call it a night. Bob said there would be wake up calls in time for us to grab a bite of breakfast before the car came to take us all to the debriefing. We all agreed, as we parted; what a day this one had been!

Chapter Twenty

Even had I *not* be in possession of that *exceptionally clear conscience*, which I possibly may have previously mentioned, I would have slept like a log. I don't think any of the rest of our crew had any trouble sleeping either. If that wakeup call had not come, I know I would likely have slept until noon. I staggered in and out of the shower and managed to get myself dressed without hardly opening my eyes. No mean trick I'll have you know. It did make shaving a trifle awkward but I managed to just peak enough to get the job done. The three of us were just a bit bleary-eyed when we gathered in the hotel dining room. Berlin Bob was waiting for us and told us the car taking us for the debriefing was already waiting out in front. He already had a carafe of steaming coffee on the table waiting for us. Good hot strong coffee sure does wonders for the spirits under these circumstances and by the second cup; all of us were once again our "sweet, jovial selves". Breakfast had already been ordered; ham and cheese omelets, sausage, toast and juice. Twenty minutes later, we were on our way. It was eight o'clock on the dot.

Golly! I hadn't expected there would be so many people. The Bobs, Henri Molier, Roberta and I were seated at a table on a slightly raised platform. In front of us were rows of folding chairs and there must have been eighteen or twenty people sitting there waiting for us. They were all police or intelligence representatives from a number of different countries. Henri Molier of Interpol, acted as a moderator. First, he had each of those attending stand, introduce themselves, state their particular responsibility and the country they represented. He then introduced those of us on the platform. He said for convenience, the de-briefing would be conducted in English.

He began by outlining how the network had first been discovered in California and then how I had wound up over here and had been drafted as an unpaid volunteer. He also explained how, Roberta and

I had discovered lists of additional clients of the escape network. He chuckled as he told how our exploits had managed to severely aggravate the network operators. .As he told in detail just what we had done at the banks he had his audience chuckling also. It was then that the idea of using us as bait began to look like a pretty good bet. Perhaps, with proper planning, more of the people involved could be gathered up. As it worked out, things turned out even better than anyone had hoped. We had put a big crimp in the network's operation.

He then explained our plan and how it had worked out. He had the names of all those we had taken in or had dispatched. He also had the names and all the information that was on the lists we had taken from the banks. There were also of course the intern-clerk at the bank and the Rent-a-Thugs that had gotten involved. All of this information would be made available to any of them that wished it. He then opened things up for questions, most of which Berlin Bob fielded. When he was asked who had set up the plan he claimed that most of the nuts and bolts of the operations were from suggestions of mine. Now, he shouldn't have said that. I said then that I was sorry but I had to interrupt. This whole operation was strictly a joint undertaking, I said. without the help of the Swiss State Police and Interpol and the coordination of everything by my friends I only knew as the Bobs, none of this would have worked. And, I pointed out also, that if it had not been for the expertise of Roberta *I* likely would not be here right now.

Roberta rose then and said she had hoped it would not be necessary for her to speak but she wanted to set the record straight. While it was true, this was a joint effort as, Deputy Thomas had said, her Deputy had been the one that saved our lives on several occasions and then she had to go into detail about those. By then, everyone seemed to have questions on various phases of the things we had done. They wanted to know from me how I had known what to do when these things happened. I said that it was all in the preplanning and calling on our previous experiences. The help of our back-up crews and the coordination of efforts by the two Bobs are what made everything work. I laughed and said that, plus the recent invention of the magical cell phones. Then I asked. How many of you already have a cell phone and most of those present raised their hands amid much general chuckling.

We spent over four hours at this and I think by then they had just about rung out every thought any of us had ever had about what had taken place the previous day. Henri said then, "Let's give our friends a break now. I think we must have covered everything we need to know in sufficient detail. We can repair to the dining room next door where a buffet has been laid on, compliments of the British Foreign Office and Interpol, International. Ah, that was welcome news. Roberta grabbed my arm and said I was to sit with her. I have had worse assignments.

It was a very delicious buffet. I enjoyed it even more because I guess everyone is through with me now. As soon as I can find out what we are going to do with Gretchen and Elke, I can be on my way home. While we were eating, I noticed someone come in and hand a large bulky envelope to Berlin Bob. I hope there are not some more assignments brewing. Even so, I am sure they could not possibly have anything to do with me. We were having some desert and coffee when Bob stood up. He said, "Before we all go our separate ways, I have a few remarks I would like you to hear."

"As you know," he began, "Deputy Thomas here has been doing all this strictly as an unpaid volunteer. I guess if he told us once he has told us a dozen times that we must never, under any circumstances, let word of what he was doing reach the ears of his wife, Grethel. If that were to happen, he assured us, she would kill him for sure. What he was doing now was not the purpose for which she had reluctantly allowed him to come here. I think he feared what his wife might do more than the people who were actually trying to kill him. I know that by now all of you know what a remarkable feat he has performed in helping to bring yesterday's operation to such a successful conclusion. If, as I have, you had talked with Agent Clarke of the FBI you would know of his other exploits, again all without pay, back in California where all this started. I think you might be truly amazed. Al Clarke thinks he is a one-man army and I think he is probably right. I know Roberta, who has seen him in operation first hand, will agree.

As you are aware our agents, when on assignment, never use their actual names. About a month ago, when all this began, we started using the code name Bob. At that time we had no idea there would wind up being so many of them. Deputy Thomas has kidded us since about all the Bob's there were and said we now had enough to form a club, pointing out we would only need one nametag we could pass around as the need arose. When you get to know him, you soon find out, he has a highly developed sense of humor. That sure has made it a pleasure for us to work with him.

We can't let word of his exploits reach his Grethel, but we "Bobs" do not intend he should leave without his knowing how we feel about him as a fellow agent and as a man. We have therefore formed the Loyal and Fraternal Order of Bobs. All of the Bobs have unanimously elected Deputy William Thomas an honorary Bob. We have had the scroll I have here prepared attesting to that fact. Having it ready in time is thanks to the expertise of Prague Bob. Each of the Bobs, using their legal names, has signed the back of the scroll. We would never do that except for a fellow Bob that we trust. I don't think that Grethel can object to a simple scroll, do you? It means however, if Deputy Bob ever needs help, he need only contact any of the Bobs and help will be forthcoming. Now Roberta, if you will drag Deputy Bob up here I can present this important document." You can imagine how all this had made me feel. I wish I had had some idea something like this had been planned.

Roberta led me over to the table where Bob was standing and he handed her the scroll to present to me. As she did this she said, "Don't forget, I am one of the Bobs also, William. If you think now that you are getting off with just a simple handshake and handing over of the scroll you are mistaken. With that, she grabbed me around the neck and gave me one of those kisses I thought only to ever get from Grethel. Of course, I was blushing then and everyone was laughing. Anyway, that gave me a little time to compose myself.

When the applause and laughter had stopped, I felt I now would be able to say a few words. "This all came about because I had to come over here to check out a couple things and try to ease my wife's unhappiness over the disappearance of her father," I told them. "Everything seemed to just kind of snowball shortly after I arrived. One thing just lead to another. I am just happy everything turned out well. I must tell you that all the Bobs I have met, including I guess my favorite Bob, Roberta, are likely the finest people I will ever meet. It distresses me greatly that two of them lost their lives, most likely because they were mistaken for Grethel and me. Maybe we evened the score a little for that but it does little to change the feeling of loss that we feel.

This beautiful scroll is going to hang in my den. Everyone on that scroll is to consider that that room is the headquarters of the Loyal and

Fraternal Order of Bobs. It is expected that anytime one of the Bobs is within striking distance of headquarters, he is honor bund to visit and see this scroll, which will be hanging there, not to honor me but them. I only wish the people of our country could know all that these fine people do for them with little or no recognition. They will get that however, when they visit our clubhouse, believe me. Thank you very much. I consider what you have done is a great honor for me. This beautiful scroll is something I shall always treasure."

The meeting broke up now and it seemed everyone had to stop by and shake my hand and offer words of congratulations. I've got to tell you, for me it was very moving and I thought was much more than my efforts warranted. When I murmured this to Roberta on our way out of the room she said, "Don't be such a Ninny, William; you deserve all those good words and more. Let us have no more foolishness. It's time now for us to get back to the hotel. You have to phone your relatives and I have to fix up my flight back to the States." Prague Bob said he would ride with us. He will be on his way back to Europe tomorrow. Roberta had to repair her make-up and Prague Bob said he had to do something similar before we caught our ride and for me to wait for them.

I was waiting in the lobby for Roberta and Prague Bob when Berlin Bob came up to me to shake my hand. "Deputy," said, "I never ever expected I was going to have the pleasure of working with a real pro when we first met at the Schonbrunn Palace. I don't know if I will ever have the opportunity to visit our clubhouse but if I don't, believe me, you are surely one Bob I will never forget." With that, he turned away and was gone. He certainly is one Bob *I* never will forget either.

CHAPTER TWENTY-ONE

BY THE TIME I was able to call the Thatchers it was two o'clock. The Major answered. It was sure good to hear his voice. He was overjoyed, he said, that I was home, safe and sound. They had all been on tenterhooks waiting to hear from me. Ethel wanted to know when I would be there as she intends to prepare a feast in celebration of my homecoming. The Major informed me he had also .laid in a supply of the Scotch I liked and he could not wait to share it with me. Gretchen and Elke couldn't wait to see me. Elke had been jumping up and down like a teenager he said, laughing. Elke must have grabbed the phone, as the next voice I heard was hers. "Oh, William, we have been so worried and thought you were never going to get here. Please say you will come tomorrow. Aunt Ethel can't wait to prepare the celebration." I said I thought I could do that and then the Major was back on the line. He said he had heard Elke and they would expect me to morrow.

I said I should be there by late afternoon if that was a good time and he said that would be just fine. I had found that Roberta's flight would not be until the following day so I asked the Major to check with Ethel and see if it was OK to bring Roberta with me. They had met her briefly at the airport when she had delivered Elke to them. He said that of course she would be more than welcome. They would look forward to getting to know her. I told him I knew Roberta would be pleased and I was looking forward to seeing them all again. A few more parting words and we hung up. I didn't intend to do one more thing for the rest of this day except catch up on my nap time. We old timers, you know, need plenty of rest.

Roberta didn't know much more about getting around London than I but we were furnished a car, courtesy of the friendly Bobs; no hassle about getting a rental this time. We even had a pretty good map to go with it; maybe why we only got slightly lost once. It was pleasant having someone to ride with me. I told Roberta about my experience during the war taking the truck convoy through the Billingsgate fish market that morning. She thought that was funny but I told her I sure did not make many friends among the fishmongers as they scattered to get out of the way of the trucks. I also told her about my adventure with my friend Singh, the Singing Sikh, a couple months earlier. When she finally stopped .laughing she said she sure wish she could have seen that.

We arrived at the Thatchers at three-thirty. We had no sooner gotten out of the car than the front door flew open; Elke raced out and flung herself at me. I almost couldn't hold her. She had her arms wrapped around my neck then and was kissing me. Roberta laughed, "Boy, Deputy, do you suppose that Elke may have missed you?" Elke was jabbering away so fast I couldn't make out a word she was saying. Then she noticed Roberta and she got a big hug also. By then the Major had come out and suggested that Else let go of us so we could all go into the house. We did, among much laughing and chattering.

Ethel and Gretchen were waiting for us and of course, there were more hugs and kisses. "Welkommen home, Wilhelm," Gretchen said. "Now you see I a little English sprechen—speak." I complemented her then on how well she was doing.

Roberta I introduced as the lady that had saved my life at least a couple times and she got hugs and kisses too. Golly, what a hugging and kissing time we were having! Roberta told me, :You know , Deputy, I kind of get the impression that these people may like you, difficult as that is to understand. She laughed along with the rest of us; what a joyful time it was!

"My boy," the Major said, "I have made special arrangements with Her Majesties Government to declare the sun over the yardarm immediately upon your arrival. Let us therefore adjourn to the salon and get comfortable. Elke piped up then with, "Major Thatcher, you should expect that William will no doubt have six or eight drinks." "By jove, a man after my own heart" he replied. "We have heard about your six or eight drinks, my boy and most likely everything else you may have ever said to Elke." Everyone was chuckling. Ethel and Gretchen then had to return to their chores in the kitchen but would return soon. "Don't talk about anythin until they got back." Roberta and Elke elected to have white wine and the Major went to his bar to prepare those and our Scotch.

As we were skipping our drinks, after suitable toasts, the major said that Gretchen and Elke had told them how I had gotten them out Berlin and away from the clutches of Bruno and his henchmen. He said that was just a "smashing" bit of work. He said it was obvious I had a natural talent for intelligence work. He had spent the last two years of his service attached to MI5 and he thought he knew an accomplished agent when he saw one. I thanked him and said I thought plain good luck had a lot to do with what had happened. He harrumphed and said, "Don't talk nonsense, my boy. I am fully aware that luck did not play a very big part; planning however, did." Ethel and Gretchen joined us and the Major went to fix their drinks.

Ethel was teaching Gretchen English, Elke told me. They were together much of the time and Gretchen was gradually acquiring a small vocabulary of English words. Elke was helping. Gretchen had said she was determined to speak well enough to make herself understood. I told Elke that her accent sounded much like American English and she said that was as she wished it. I guess this was as good a time as any to find out what they wanted to do. They were both vehement that they did not want to go back to Berlin. They were positive now that their father and husband had been killed by Bruno or some one of the Stasi at his behest, all to put Elke in a position where she would be vulnerable. They said they shuddered whenever they thought what could have happened if I had not appeared when I did. I said I would do what I could to help them.

The Major said then, "My boy, I do believe it must be time for the next of those six or eight drinks don't you? Then, we must hear what adventures you had after you had delivered Elke to us. I am fairly certain we have heard everything that you may have done or said up to that time perhaps, six or eight times. He and Ethel laughed. I get the impression they are pretty pleased with their niece. As the drinks were handed out, Roberta said perhaps it would be better if she took over here. Knowing her Deputy, as she did, she knew he would leave out many of the most interesting details where he was involved.

Well, you all know about that stuff. The Major, Ethel, Gretchen and Elke apparently seemed to find it all interesting. At any rate, they were all giving Robert their rapt attention. From time to time Elke translated for her mother. An hour later, she had finished and had also answered some questions from the Major. Ethel said then, "William, I can't believe you and Roberta could do all those things." I said, "Well I'll tell you, without Roberta, I am quite certain they would not have been done at all." Roberta snorted, "Let me tell you folks, there are a few people who have actually seen my favorite deputy in action and have referred to him as a one man army. I think they may be right; even if he did almost shoot my ear off one time." She laughed then and added that it had not seemed at all funny at the time however.

I told them then, please remember, not one word of any this is ever to reach Grethel's ears. This was not the reason she had consented to my coming here at all. I had said this was just a simple job that should take only few days and I had promised not to "get into any mischief". One thing however just seemed to lead to another. I was pretty sure now that once I got home, I seriously doubted that I would ever leave the house again. Everyone laughed and Ethel then said OK, if anyone wanted just one more short drink now was the time.

The ladies all opted to attend to matters in the kitchen and dining room and the Major and I agreed that perhaps just a short one would be in order for us. We sat in companionable silence a few minutes as we enjoyed the excellent Scotch the Major had provided. Finally, the Major cleared his throat. He said then, "You cannot know, William, how much I value having met you and having you now as one of our family." I told him that I also greatly appreciated getting to know all of them. I felt very comfortable being here. Perhaps it was because we had shared some similar wartime experiences. He said that possibly was the case, in any event, he wanted me to know how very proud he was of me and of my accomplishments. Elke coming to announce dinner was ready then saved me from further embarrassment.

It was a most festive dinner; complete with wines appropriate for the different courses. As we were having desert and coffee, Roberta remarked to me that we had both been invited to spend the night here with the Thatchers. It had looked like there could be a problem providing enough beds but a decision had finally been made that solved that problem; as Elke and she had both been wives of mine from time to time, the three of us could just share the large bed and that had solved that problem. Elke said it did seem to be a most reasonable solution."Wasn't it nice that we could stay for the night?" Roberta said, "Anyway, William, I always did want to cuddle with you. "I did also," Elke added; but we must be sure that before he gets into bed, Roberta, he takes his shoes off. He does seem to be forgetful about that at times"

I was sitting there with my mouth opening and closing without being able to make a sound. I guess I looked like a beached guppy. Everyone sat there looking at me seriously. Elke finally said, "I do hope you will stay, William. Do you think it too early for us to get ready to go to bed?" I was dumbfounded. I guess then they finally had had enough fun and they all burst out in gales of laughter. Everyone but the Major had been in on this. Then Roberta said, "Remember, William, I told you two days ago I would think of *something* before we parted. You should have seen the expression on your face. Really though William, would sleeping with Elke and me be such a horrifying experience?" When I could finally get my wits, what was left of them, together, I said that it just was not fair when two experienced women of the world ganged up on a poor naïve country boy. I was going to tell on them to Grethel, *then* they would be very sorry. Roberta said, "Naïve Country Boy, hah, who do you think you are kidding?"

Well, it was time for us to get back to the hotel. Roberta was flying out tomorrow and had things she must do. I have to make my arrangements as well. I would return here the next day so we could discuss Gretchen and Elke's situation. Then I must be on my way or I know Grethel and Elaine will for sure, come and get me. On the way back to London, Roberta told me that the Bobs would see to my transportation just let them know when I wanted to leave. As we parted to enter our rooms, she gave me one of "those" kisses and said, "Now, you just be careful out there by yourself, Deputy." Golly-----I just have to get out of here---and soon!

Boy oh boy! Now you've got to read:

Part Two------"G! Ityk Iwok

(Polish? Perhaps--Bulgarian? could it possibly even be *HUNGARIAN*??)

Part Two
*G! Ityk; Iwok!

Do you think that could perchance be Polish? Possibly Hungarian??

I Hope you have read, "Good Heavens Miss Evans" and finished Part One, "One Thing Just Lead to Another", before you start this story. If not, you are going to be a little confused about what is happening.

CHAPTER ONE

THE BOBS DID ALL right by me on my transportation home. It still seems like a hell of a long, boring plane ride though from London to LAX, even with the best of arrangements. We landed in LA at ten PM and by then I was bushed. No point in trying to get home tonight so I got a room at the airport hotel and I was out like a light as soon as I got close to the pillow.

I didn't leap out of bed at dawn either. I was going to start living a normal life style from now on. After a good shower, I went down to the coffee shop and had me a nice leisurely and substantial breakfast while I read the morning LA Times. After all the driving around we had been doing the last couple of weeks, I just did not feel up to another five-hour drive to get home. I began checking into the possibility of a charter flight and got lucky. The Sierras had been getting snow for a couple weeks and the ski resorts were open. There now were daily flights to Mammoth for the skiers and ski-bunnies. Thank goodness, it was the middle of the week and they were only half booked. With a little fast-talking and an extra fifty dollars, they agreed to let me off in Bishop. None of the other passengers objected to the extra ten minutes travel time. The extra take-off and landing didn't use fifty dollars of gas so I guess everyone was happy. We should depart in an hour and twenty minutes.

I found a phone and called home to alert them I would soon be on my way. Good, Grethel was home. When she heard it was I she shrieked, "William, I thought you were never coming home again. We will be at the airport to meet you; and William dear, do not expect to get out of the house again for at least a month." I laughed and told her, "I think my dear Grethel that I might not ever go *outside* again." I said perhaps we could make an exception on a rare occasion and pop over to the country club for a meal. Other than that, I expected I was going to become a recluse. She laughed and told me to hurry up and come home but don't be surprised if she seemed a little heavier than the last time I saw her.

Chapter Two

WE CLIMBED OUT OF LAX, out over the Pacific following the regular takeoff pattern, and then headed easterly toward the San Gabriel Mountains. Fifteen minutes later, we were looking down at Baldy and the Cajon Pass. The north slopes of the San Gabriel and San Bernardino Mountains already have a little snow. It sure was nice to be home where you could recognize a few familiar landmarks.

At around one hundred and fifty miles an hour, it does not take too long to make it to Bishop. They didn't exactly throw me and my bags off the plane while it was still moving but they sure didn't waste time. I barely had time to get out of the way and they were taxiing down to the end of the runway to take off again. Another ten minutes and they will be at the Mammoth landing strip.

Strange, no Grethel, no Elaine, what's going on here? I was struggling to pick up the bags and all the packages I had when a Deputy Sheriff approached me and said, "Maybe I can give you a hand with those, Deputy." I said, "Thank you very much, Deputy, it sure looks like I could use a little help. I was expecting some of my family here to meet me but it appears they have been delayed." He said that was his understanding. Sergeant, Miller had asked him to come by and ferry me home. No problems he said, just a slight change of plans apparently. We got all my stuff into the squad car and took off for the place we had rented.

"Boy, the old town sure looks good," I remarked to the Deputy. "I may never leave again." He chuckled and said it was an all-right place he guessed but he would like to see something else once in a while. I said no doubt he would have a chance to do that one of these days. In a few minutes, we had arrived at the house and my friend helped me haul my stuff up to the door where he left me; he had to get back on patrol and would no doubt be seeing me around town. I rang the doorbell a couple times but there was no answer. I sure hope Grethel had not had to go to the doctor's. I fished out my keys, opened the door, piled all my stuff inside and closed the door. I wonder where Grethel could be. I went to the front room to see if there could be a note she had left for me. Strange, all the drapes were drawn.

Just as I went through the door, an arm went around my neck and another around my waist. If I had still been in Europe I likely would have had a seizure just about now. "Welcome, home my darling William," Grethel said, followed by one of those kisses for which she is so famous. At the same time, there were shouts of, "Surprise!, Surprise!, Welcome Home!" All the lights came on then. I could see now why all the blinds were shut in the middle of the afternoon. There was a welcome home banner hung on the wall of the living room and decorations of balloons and streamers all over. Someone sure had done a lot of work in a hurry.

There were Elaine and Al and also Verne and Francine. What a nice surprise. I'm glad now I had stayed in LA the night before and got rested so I could enjoy this get-together. I got a hug and Kiss from Elaine of course and I told her what a nice person she was; I knew she had helped Grethel do all the decorating. I thought it all looked beautiful. Grethel said that actually Elaine had done most of the work. Everyone was talking at once and it was a very festive time indeed. Verne said then, "You are all going to be Francine and my guests at the club for dinner tonight. They are icing the champagne even as we speak. It seems to me however, the sun must be sufficiently over the yardarm somewhere so that we can indulge in a libation of some sort before heading out. What do you think, Al?" Al said, believing that such a situation might arise he had already laid out supplies and equipment for just such an occasion in the kitchen. I said, "Great, Let us all repair to yon kitchen, I do believe I may have my usual six or eight drinks just to get the evening off to a good start." Grethel was of course being a good girl and had just some good old California orange juice. By the time we were ready to leave for dinner, we were all in a jovial mood. I asked Elaine if she was now ready to hear the yodeling I had learned in the Alps. She pretended to be gagging of course and said, "Please, please, not before dinner, Bill." I remonstrated, "Doesn't everyone know yet, I sign like a veritable thrush?" We all climbed into our various cars and off we went.

Everyone had a great time. There were a lot of people we knew having dinner at the club. Many of them stopped by to say they were glad to see I was home safe and sound. Boy, it sure was nice to be back home! I swear Grethel looked even prettier than when I had left. I whispered that in her ear as I held her chair for her. I won't tell her what the Bobs had uncovered about her father until we are alone. I suspect however, she knows what is coming. If her father had been alive, I would have told her that before now.

I told everyone about meeting Grethel's Aunt and Uncle Thatcher and part of my escapade with Singh the Singing Sikh. That was good for a laugh. Al told everyone he couldn't give a lot of details because much of it was still classified but he said, "Our one-man army," as he insists on calling me, "was up to his old tricks. They are still counting up the number of the *Network Gang* that are now out of commission, one way or another, due to Bill's activities the last couple weeks. So far it looks to be at least twelve or thirteen."

He said that how I tricked Bruno and got Elke and her mother out of Berlin and out his clutches was *not* classified information and he could tell them of that. Well, he got the facts pretty straight and he sure did have their attention. He must have had some conversations with Berlin Bob. When I asked, he said that yes, they had had talked some. He went on to say, that was one CIA Agent who was now a good friend of mine. I said I felt I was friends of *all* the agents I had been working with. *They* were the ones really responsible for any of the successes we were able to achieve. Al said he knew it was joint effort but my friends in the CIA were giving me a lot of credit for the success they, Interpol and the local police had had.

All during this time, Grethel had not said a word. She had a kind of speculative look on her face I noticed. Thank goodness, he could not go into a lot of detail or I am sure Grethel would have been mad at me. It had been a grand evening but it was finally time to call it quits. After thanking Francine and Verne for a fine dinner, we all went our separate ways.

As we were walking out Verne said I might stop by the office tomorrow when I had time. I could write up my final report and maybe then, he could let me revert to my honorary position. He wasn't quite sure yet how that was going to work out until we could talk to the sheriff. Tommy Archer had been making noises about keeping me on even if they had to *pay* me a little something. I asked Verne if he thought I should sic Grethel on him but he said he hoped that was not going to be necessary. Anyway, we could talk about that when I came to the office.

Boy! It was sure nice to spend a night in my own house in my own bed, with a girl who really *was* my wife. I didn't think it was a good idea right then to explain why it was necessary for the play-acting of Elke and Roberta. It is all just too complicated. I am sure any attempt to explain all that happened was only going to get me in more trouble than I suspect I am already in. Grethel always professes to being a very broad minded person however, I suspect that does not entirely extend to me.

It was a little while before I could get going in the morning. Grethel explained that I had a considerable amount of catching-up to do to make up for all the time I had been away from her. She figured it would be several days, at least, before I had made amends for being away from her for such a long time. I said that of course that was going to cut into the time I had planned to spend on all the accumulated chores awaiting my attention. I was prepared however to make any sacrifice necessary if that would please her. She asked if it was necessary for her to punch my arm again and I told her I would really try to do my best to behave.

After phoning the office and telling them the time I would be there, I fixed up a big breakfast with all the things we like. Grethel sat at the kitchen table to keep me company while I was doing the fixing. She said it was just like the old times back up a Lundy. It sure was nice. I had gotten pretty tired of eating out and enjoyed getting our breakfast again.

When we finished eating, I figured this was as good a time as any and gave Grethel the letter her father had written. She spent a little time reading and rereading it then said she had been expecting something like this but nevertheless, it was a blow. I told her I understood and held her and petted her until she had finally finished crying.

We sat then while I had a refill on my coffee and Grethel had another glass of orange juice. I told her what the Bobs had been able to discover from their informants. It wasn't pleasant information but I thought she would rather know her father had not had to suffer torture at the hands of the Stasi. She said that was true and she should thank the men who had gone to all that trouble. I told her I had already done that. I knew it would not make her less sad, I told her but it was very likely that at least some of those responsible had been among the ones we had taken care of in the past couple weeks. Grethel said she appreciated my being frank with her; this was a sadness she would just have to live through. She loved me for finding the truth for her. "My William always does for me just what he says he would do." she said. (How could I not?) Ah, another nice hug and kiss.

Grethel told me to go off for my meeting at the Sheriff's office; she would clean up the kitchen. She would just like to be alone for a little while right now. I guess I am still on active duty so I put on all my stuff and drove down town. I should be a good old private citizen very soon.

Well everyone at the office seemed glad to see me. It did seem like I was back home. Verne was waiting for me and said, "let's go into the Sheriff's office and talk." The county seat of course is in Lone Pine but the largest concentrations' of people in the area are in and around Bishop and Mammoth so the Sheriff spends a lot his time in the office here. Talk about surprises, Al Clarke was there, as well as the Sheriff. I said, "Why do I have the feeling I am going to hear something I really don't want to hear?" "Probably because we have some information you might find disturbing," Sheriff Archer said. "I'll let Al here fill you in on the details."

Al didn't mince any words, Gretchen and Elke were both in the hospital in England and in serious condition. Two men in a car had tried to force them off the road as they were driving from their apartment to visit the Thatchers. Gretchen had just recently started to learn to drive and this was to be a practice run. Her injury was the most serious. If not for the fact both ladies had been wearing seat belts, they might not have survived the crash. The two men in the car causing the crash attempted to drag Elke from the car but two men in a car following, who had witnessed what happened, rushed over and the two men fled.

Both women were unconscious when they were taken to the hospital and it was a day before the Thatchers found out what had happened. When they had not arrived as scheduled, the Major had immediately started enquiries. Of course, when Elke had regained consciousness she had the hospital contact Major Thatcher. He and Ethel had gone to the hospital immediately. She told them that just before losing consciousness she thought she recognized Bruno as one of the two men trying to drag her from the car. She wasn't positive however and could not swear that it was really he.

Damn! I was afraid something like this might happen when I learned Bruno had escaped apprehension in Berlin. I guess it had not been too smart telling him the ladies were going to visit relatives in England. What could he hope to gain by kidnapping Elke at this time?

Al went on to say that from the lists Roberta and I had uncovered plus the treasure trove of letters we had gotten in Reno it seemed that friend Bruno was very heavily involved in the escape network. It appears he was responsible for the disappearance of a number of others beside Gretchen's husband. The German Government was researching the Stasi records they had been able to confiscate before they, the Stasi, had destroyed all of them. It is their intention to prosecute all those involved in murders and atrocities. Old Bruno has good cause to be very nervous about his future.

I told Verne and Al how Bruno kept hinting to me that he hoped to see me in California and that he might be bringing a lady-friend with him. He didn't know at the time that I was planning on spiriting Gretchen and Elke out from under his nose and out of Germany.

I speculated that maybe it was not such a good idea for me to revert to my inactive status just at the moment. Al and the Sheriff smiled and said that was just what they had been about to suggest. They were happy we were all thinking the same way. Were we ever going to be rid of these people? They were like cockroaches; it seemed you just could not exterminate all of them. I said I had to go home and fill Grethel in on the latest development and then put through a call to Major Thatcher. I sure hoped he still has some connections with the people in MI5 or MI6.

Grethel was aghast when she heard what had happened to her aunt and her cousin. "William, have you thought of a plan to help them?" she asked. She sure does expect a lot of me. I said I was not sure what I could do from this far away but she said she was sure that I would think of something. We did not need these bad people to harm any more of her family. If there was any way she could help, she wanted me to know she would do whatever she could; just as long as it did not jeopardize any of my numerous children. She chuckled, threw her arms around me and gave me one of *those* kisses. Well that would have given me an incentive if I ever needed one. I still need to think of something however. Maybe it will come to me while I am discussing this with the Major.-----I hope.

It was almost eight PM when my call went through. Ethel was so glad I had called. They were going to phone me but the Major had been so busy at the hospital he had not yet had time. He had been there most of the last two days and she had been several times as well. Gretchen was still in intensive care but Elke likely would be released before long if she continued to improve. I asked Ethel to have the Major call me collect whenever he got home and she said that she would tell him.

I had the glimmering of an idea now and wanted to run it by the Major. Maybe we could fool Bruno one more time. I was sure Elke had not been mistaken when she thought he might have been one of her attempted kidnappers. It was very likely that he had also been responsible for the death of her father if he had not caused it himself. I was certain he had become obsessed with her. I think that likely he had gotten pretty well used to having anything he wanted his way while the Communists and the Stasi were running the country. He could just not stand not having things his way yet again.

The Major's call came through forty-five minutes later. He was so glad to be able to speak with me he said. He apologized for not calling me sooner but he had been concerned that Bruno or his confederates might make another try for Elke or her mother. He too was convinced that Bruno had to be one of those involved. It was a little hard to know what their intentions could be. Was it just to capture Elke or were they just intent on avenging Bruno's previous humiliation? The Major still had some friends from his old Intel days and they had set in place a little surreptitious surveillance plan at the hospital. Did I have any thoughts on what else he might do?

I asked if there had been anything in the newspapers about the accident and he said not as far as he had seen. I said then that perhaps an article might soon appear in the news about the recent accident involving two women from Berlin. Both were now in the hospital in very critical condition. Perhaps they might also soon die. I, of course, must then come over for the funeral arrangements. Grethel would want her aunt and cousin buried in America where they would be near her. She might possibly accompany me on this sad occasion, as they had no family left in Europe. Did the Major think I might have the germ of an idea here?

The Major chuckled and said, "You are a genius my boy. By Jove! This is like the good old days! It will work. I will start on the preliminaries tomorrow. I still have a few connections, thank goodness. I will phone you when things are under way and give you the gen on the arrangements." I told him I was pretty sure he could handle everything on his end quite well and would wait to hear the further developments.

I told Grethel what I was thinking and how I thought we might work it to see what she thought. I had not told her before that Elke looked very much like her. I planned on using that one more time. She said maybe with the help of my friends it might work. It certainly seemed worth a try. Why not see what Al might think of the idea. I found Al at Elaine's. (My, what a surprise.) He would be at the Sheriff's office tomorrow morning he said and would like to hear what I had come up with. Then he was on his way back to San Francisco.

The Sheriff was in Sacramento so it was just Al, Verne and I that met the next morning. I told them of my conversation with Major Thatcher and how I thought we might extract Elke and Gretchen out of England. Both agreed that with the right preparation and timing it should work. Al agreed to contact the Bobs still working the project to let them know I was back on the job and why. I asked he also have them ask Roberta to contact Major Thatcher who she had already met. I was pretty sure we were going to have need of her expertise later on to make this work.

Our local paper was about to put out its weekly edition so I popped over there and had them include an item about the relatives of Grethel's that had been killed in a terrible auto accident in England. The article went on to say that it was likely that the Mayor and Mrs. Thomas must journey to England to see about arrangements for transporting the remains here for burial. OK, that part is done, now to explain to Grethel her part of the plan.

CHAPTER THREE

TWO DAYS LATER GRETHEL and I were on our way to LA. No one else knew it but she was staying with my brother in Claremont. I took a plane from Ontario to Washington where I met briefly with the task force working on the escape network project. They were wondering if there were any of that group still out there as it seemed I must have gotten most of them out of the way one way or another. I said I was afraid there were still some out there. I knew of two for sure in England at that very moment. I hoped they had found most of those that had made their way into this country and they said they had been quite successful so far. As I had requested, Roberta was scheduled to meet with Major Thatcher very soon, likely tomorrow morning.

They put me up for the night and had me a space on the shuttle in the morning for La Guardia. I had a seat on the *Concorde* from there to London. Well, well, I guess it doesn't hurt to have friends in high places, does it? So far, everything seems to be going just as the Major and I had laid it out.

It wasn't too many hours and we were making our approach into Heathrow. Let us hope now that everything goes according to plan. With the Major and Roberta handling things there, I'm pretty confident everything is going to be in order. I will know for sure in about thirty minutes. We taxied up to the terminal and the covered jet-way finally moved out and up to the door of the SST. I am scheduled to be first off and my seat was right by the door as had been planned.

Finally, the door opened, I stepped through and Grethel took my arm. The flight attendant standing there said, "I hope you had a pleasant flight, Mr. and Mrs. Thomas." Grethel answered, "Oh yes indeed. It was very enjoyable. Thank you very much." We proceeded then along the jet-way and the concourse and into the terminal where people had gathered to meet arrivals. The Major and Ethel were there, looking suitably grave as the occasion warranted. There were only a few words spoken and we went to claim our luggage and thereafter drove out to the Thatcher's place in Twyford. There was not much conversation during the ride either. I am not ever going to complain about driving the Southern California Freeways again. I'm glad this trip was the major's job. It sure did require all his attention. We were unlucky enough to hit one of the peak traffic times.

We finally made it and the Major put up the car as we made our way inside where he soon joined us. His first words were, "Egad, I think I am getting too old to drive in this horrendous traffic. Would anyone mind if we called a halt here and I fix us a little something that will calm my nerves?" I said I sure thought he deserved something. I was just thankful that he was the one doing the driving. I didn't think I could have done it. I would have been a basket case for sure before we ever got out of the city. As he went to work at his little bar, he said that Roberta would be by soon. She had stayed behind until all passengers had left. She wanted to see if anyone was hanging around watching the passengers. The Major said there also was an old friend of his who was doing the same thing from a somewhat different vantage point, a man with much experience in this sort of thing.

It was just about then the telephone rang. It was the Major's friend calling from the airport. He was about to head for home but wanted to report in first. There had been two men, obviously not passengers, who were closely watching all the passengers arrive. He noticed that when Grethel and I had left with the Thatchers they had left also. He followed and saw them take a taxi. He had the number of the taxi and tomorrow would find out where it had left the two men. The Major thanked him and asked him to let him know what he found out the next day. "Just an excellent chap, Alf," he told us, "Was one for our very best men and tickled to death to get back in the harness again. We can rely on him."

A half hour later, Roberta arrived. Golly, it was good to see her again! I got a big hug. She figured she had earned a Scotch by now too and the Major hustled over to his bar to take care of her. We all sat back then and I guess had a collective sigh of relief. The first phase of our plan seemed to have gone OK. I asked Roberta then how she had worked her part.

She and Elke, in their flight attendant uniforms and trundling their little flight cases, moved on down the concourse we would be using. As the plane taxied up to the terminal, they were moving along the jet-way as it moved out to meet the plane. Elke slipped her flight attendant's jacket into the traveling case and slipped on the slightly padded Grethel dress. Her case would be fastened onto Roberta's when she left. As the plane door opened, she stepped from behind Roberta and took my arm just as I came out. It looked like she had just stepped off the plane with me. I really think the people behind me were sure she had been on the plane with me, especially when they heard Roberta ask if we had enjoyed the flight. I told them both what a great job they had done. now to move on to the next phase of our plan.

While we were having our drink, Elke told me how her mother had been forced off the road. Now that she had recovered and had time to think back, she was sure, it *had* been Bruno that had been trying to pry her out of the car. Her mother was still in serious condition but there was now no doubt that she would in time, fully recover.

The Major then explained how they had "died" and been moved to the hospital morgue. Among the recent deaths at the hospital, there were two that looked enough like them they could be used for that purpose for a day or two. We would visit the morgue tomorrow and arrange to have the remains airlifted to the US. It was probably well to do all this as expeditiously as possible.

Roberta had gotten a room for "Grethel" and me where she was staying so we three took our leave of the Thatchers, having made arrangements to meet tomorrow morning at the morgue. When we got to our room, Elke said it was nice being married to me again. She was only sorry that her "condition" required we have separate beds. When she saw my expression, she burst out laughing----again. I will never catch on will I? We had arranged to meet with Roberta for a bite of supper a little later and that was it for today. Tomorrow we will be busy.

Chapter Four

"Grethel" and I met the Thatchers at the hospital at ten the next morning and were escorted to the morgue. We identified the bodies as those of Gretchen and her daughter, Elke. We informed the morgue that the next day the mortuary we had selected would arrive to take charge of the bodies and arrange for their shipment to the US. After we had completed the necessary paperwork, we departed and went in search of a quiet place to get some .lunch and go over the rest of the plan.

The things Elke and her mother had brought with them had already been turned over to the mortuary people. (One often used by the Major's former "friends" for similar purposes.) They would fill the caskets with those and ship them air freight to San Francisco. Al would retrieve them there and would arrange for storage until needed. There will be a brief Memorial Service at the Thatchers regular church tonight with both caskets present. "Grethel" and I leave tomorrow morning for home.

Gretchen, in the meantime, has been moved by the Major's "friends" to a different hospital. She of course is registered there under a different name. The substitute corpses will be returned to their rightful places while the shift is changing in the hospital morgue. The Major has covered all the bases and done so very well. We have all been behaving, whenever in public, as would any recently bereaved people. If Bruno, or any of his watchers, were to see us, we must portray the roles of mourning relatives. Elke was complaining about her pregnant Grethel costume as being too warm but I told her not to; she looked just as Grethel had when I had said goodbye to her in California, just as we wanted.

There were only a few of the friends of the Thatchers at the church service. The Major's friend "Alf", the watcher, was among those present. As we were exiting the church, he nodded to the Major. Shortly after we pulled away from the church, the Major's cell phone buzzed and he pulled over to the side of the road. It was Alf. He said the same two men who had been watching at the airport had been sitting in a car outside the church. They had seen us all enter and had then driven away. The cab driver who had picked them up at the airport had told him he had dropped them off at the entrance to the Underground so he had not found where they had gone. He would see what else he might be able to discover and would contact him if he were to develop anything new.

I told the Major we needed the best possible description of these two. I knew what Bruno looked like but if there were other members of the conspiracy, I would like to be able to spot them also. The major passed on this request then chuckled as he turned off his cell phone. He asked did I think photos of the men in question would satisfy my requirements. Alf would deliver them to me at the airport the next morning. The major said, "I told you, Alf was one of the best. Now you know why I could say that." Ethel had a cold supper prepared at their house and that is where we went next.

As we were having drinks before diner and chatting, the Major said he had not realized until now how he missed the excitement he had left behind when he had retired. Ethel remarked he was just like an old warhorse when the trumpets began to sound. I said that from what I had been able to observe he must have done one hell of a job when he was on active duty. Ethel said she knew that he had done a *damn* good job and she had always been so very proud of him. The Major of course harrumphed, muttered something, and said he did think it was time to have just one more drink before we ate.

I said, "You do know, "Grethel" my dear, that in your delicate condition likely you should eschew imbibing alcoholic beverages. "My dear William," She replied, "I wasn't planning on "chewing" anything. I am however not averse to *sipping* a little white wine." The Major chuckled and said he was sure he could manage that. As he passed out the drinks he remarked, "You know my boy, it is going to be dreadfully dull around here when you leave. I swear, if I were younger I might see if I could be re-called. Ethel snorted and said he could get that idea out of his head right now and with that, we all rose and went in to supper.

CHAPTER FIVE

WE WERE ALL AT the airport an hour before departure as required. The Major soon spotted Alf and a few minutes later, when he visited the men's room Alf was waiting for him. He had a small envelope in his coat pocket when he rejoined us. Elke/Grethel and I were all checked in so we went to the VIP lounge to wait for our flight to be called and to inspect the photos. They didn't look at all familiar to me but the Major was sure he had seen them somewhere before. I put them in my jacket pocket. Later I will study them again and try to commit them to memory.

It is still a long, boring ride back to California. It was a little more bearable with Elke there to talk to. She had many questions, as this was her first trip to the US. I asked that she try to be careful and act as if she had been here before. We don't know whether or not someone had been put on board to watch us. I told her I was thinking of starting the Thomas school for aspiring thespians when I had some spare time. Finally, we landed at Ontario. I sure am glad we did not have to go in at LAX. We had changed planes and gone through customs in New York.

My brother met us at the airport. You should have seen the expression on his face when he first spotted Elke. I'll bet his jaw must have dropped a foot. I said, "Thanks for meeting us, George. You do remember Grethel do you not? After all you were at our wedding weren't you?" When he could speak he gasped, "My god Bill, This is unbelievable! Grethel told us your plan but this is absolutely amazing! I can't wait to get home and for Patsy to see Elke. I said I suspected that Grethel was .likely going to be even more surprised.

Of course Elke was still wearing her Grethel costume when we got to George and Patsy's home. Patsy and Grethel were as astounded as George had been. Now seeing Elke and Grethel together, it was even hard for me to tell which was which. Elke said then would we please excuse her while she changed into some regular clothes. She had been wearing this costume so long she was even beginning to *feel* she was expecting.

When she returned she had not only changed clothes but had added an attractive wig of a light brown shade. She said she had decided that later on she was going to have her hair dyed to match that color. Grethel said she thought that was an excellent idea. She did not want William to get confused on who was who. I noted she was not smiling when she made this pronouncement. Have I made another problem for myself? George said he was taking us all out for dinner so it was time for me to get myself cleaned up and we would get under way.

It had been a long day and I was really ready for an early *goodnight*. George and patsy have plenty of room now that all their children have grown and left the nest so there was no problem with the sleeping arrangements. I think I could have slept leaning up against a wall. Grethel however wanted to *talk*. Mostly about Elke as it turned out. Finally I said, "Look my dear Grethel, Elke is extremely pretty but as far as I am concerned no one can ever be as pretty as you." She murmured, "You are a very good boy, William." She gave me another of those kisses and I was out like the proverbial light. I believe I may have previously mentioned that clear conscience business, have I not?

CHAPTER SIX

WE GOT A FAIRLY early start the next day, drove out over Cajon Pass and got on to the 395, North, not far past the summit. We were in Cramer Junction by nine and stopped for a little something to eat. I pointed out to Grethel, this was where I had breakfast that day I had met her and her companions in Bishop for dinner, so long ago it seems.. I had been here a number of times over the years. We arrived home in time for dinner and Elaine had us come to the Roadrunner and have dinner with her. Just like the good old times.

We had left Elke with George and Patsy for a few weeks. It seemed best we travel separately just in case there might be anyone keeping tabs on us. I had not been able to spot anyone but I knew if any pros had been on the job, I never would have been able to spot them.

I had copies made of the pictures Alf had taken and given some to Al and to Verne. Verne had them distributed with instructions to be on the lookout for anyone looking like either of them. I thought we had gotten Elke out pretty much undetected. With any luck we are home free. Let us hope so.

It has been decided that Elke will be staying here with her cousin, Elaine. She is cousin, *Elvira*. Grethel had picked the name. I think it just possible that our Grethel is just a teensy bit jealous.

Elvira wanted something to do so Elaine put her to work at the Roadrunner. It wasn't more than a few days later that all the single men in town seemed to find reason to call at the Roadrunner for lunch or dinner I told Elaine she probably owed Elke a percentage on all the new business she has brought in. Had she noted how the number of customers dropped way down on the days Elke did not work?

Elke was having a great time. With her new darker hair, she looked even sexier than when she was a blond. I was careful not to make that observation aloud in Grethel's company. She could have dates every night of the week if she had wanted. I think she has been taken to see all of the places of interest in and around town several times over the past few weeks. If the truth were to be told, I have a sneaking suspicion that both Elaine and Grethel are just a tad jealous. Do not expect me to say anything like *that* out loud either. I may be getting older but so far, I am not entirely senile------quite yet.

CHAPTER SEVEN

I CAN'T BELIEVE HOW much time has passed since Grethel and I had been climbing around up in the mountains. When I mentioned this at breakfast Grethel said she had a fairly good idea how long that had been when she looked down at her stomach. I suggested she might feel more comfortable spending winter at my house down south. We could do that if she wished as my tenant had just vacated. She said no, she was satisfied right here. We had made all the arrangements at our local hospital and this was where she wanted to be.

Guess who has taken up skiing? Elvira is off to the slopes whenever she has time off, either at Mammoth or June Lake. Everyone now knows about Cousin Elvira, "The Queen of the Slopes." I guess she has had about a hundred marriage proposals by now. She is making up for all that time she was stuck in East Berlin and fending off Bruno and his friends

We have gotten a phone call from the Major. Gretchen has almost completely recovered. She hoped to be able to rejoin her daughter before long. He and his adopted daughter, "Roberta", were working on plans. When all the plans were finalized, he would give us the details. I guess the Major and Roberta are kindred spirits. The Thatchers do not have any children and Roberta seems to fit right in.

It looks .like we must have done a good job with Elke. At any rate, Verne says they have not spotted anyone that looks suspicious around the city. Verne has agreed that I might just as well be inactive again----at last until they can find a new nest of bad guys that needs cleaning out. Always the kidder.

CHAPTER EIGHT

IT LOOKS LIKE THIS must be the day. Grethel told me to get the car out and the bag she had already packed. We went to the hospital to check in. Grethel said she understood it was quite the modern thing for the father to be present in the delivery room but she was not modern. I *would be notified* when all was in readiness for me to be received. Was that agreed? I said that it was. The doctor came out after I had been sitting in the waiting room for a while and said it would be a little time yet. If I wished, I could go home and they would phone me when I should return. I could see Grethel then for just a few minutes. She assured me all was going according to plan and it would be all right for me to go home for a while. She would wait right there for me. So far, it doesn't appear I have too much to say about what is going on. I drove back home.

After pacing the floor near the telephone for a couple hours, I could stand it no longer. I telephoned the hospital. They assured me that Mrs. Thomas was doing quite well. Well, OK, I guess. It occurred to me I had not had any lunch so I put a piece of lunchmeat between slices of bread. One bite and I threw it in the trash. Tasted like garbage.

About four o'clock I phoned Elaine. She was so excited. She had not known Grethel had gone to the delivery room already. I told her I was about to climb the walls soon, waiting around for the phone to ring. I was now sure that something must be going wrong. This was just too long. Now she was worried too. I said that I wouldn't mind having a little company about now and she said she would be with me soon. She said she would first stop by the hospital to see what she could learn.

Finally, at six o'clock she showed up at the door. She greeted me with, "Not to worry, Bill. Everything is going just as expected. I even had a word with Grethel. I am to tell you not to worry and then take you out for a drink and some dinner.. I have my cell phone and the hospital has my number. They can reach us if necessary. Grab your jacket and let's go. We'll take my car." Well, maybe a drink did help. The second helped a little more. That will be enough. I must keep a clear head. I really wasn't hungry but Elaine insisted I have a small diner salad and a cup of soup. Then we had a cup of coffee and Elaine said it was such a special night we should add a B&B.

It was eight when we got back to the house and by now, I was worried. Elaine said she would check with the hospital. She came back soon and said the hospital said that everything seemed to be on track and they would phone me in time. She turned on the television and we looked at that for an hour but I'll be darned if I could comprehend what was going on. It must have been some foreign language program.

At nine o'clock, the phone rang and I thought I might have a heart attack. Elaine told me to calm down; she would answer the phone. She thanked whoever it was and then said, "O.K. Bill, it is time to go over to the hospital now. We will take my car." I'm glad she offered. I'm not sure I could remember how to start mine. It seemed to take hours but I guess it was only a few minutes and we were at the hospital parking lot. Elaine kept hold of my arm and we went inside.

We were directed to the same waiting room where I had been before. We sat there for a good fifteen minutes and I said to Elaine, "I thought they said everything had been taken care of. What can be wrong now? Elaine said not to worry they had just wanted to give me enough time to get to the hospital. She was sure we would hear very soon. She sat next to me and patted my hand, murmuring all the while that I was not to worry.

I was just about a basket case at twenty to ten when the door to the section that held the delivery rooms opened. A nurse wearing a surgical mask came out, looked around and asked if there was a Mr. Thomas present. I was able to croak out a feeble, "here," and stagger to my feet. She crooked her finger at me and I followed her down the hall and into the room that she indicated. As I went through the door, she clapped a surgical mask on me muttering, "Who knows what germs you are breathing out."

There was my beloved Grethel and she was smiling at me. I was so relieved that I almost burst into tears. She was all right! She held out her hands to me and said that maybe if I came over and moved that mask just a little maybe she could have a little kiss. That I could do. At that moment, Elaine came into the room carrying a big bunch of red roses. She said, "Poor Bill has been so worried, Ellie, he hasn't been able to think. I did what any good Godmother should do and I had these ready for him to give you." Now we all did have tears and I had a big hug and kiss for Elaine. What a nice person she is!

The nurse who had been observing all this said, "If you are all through with this little reunion, perhaps Mr. Thomas would like to see what his family looks like now." Gosh, I had forgotten why we were here. She left and was back in minutes and put a little bundle in a pink blanket in my arms. Grethel said, "And that, William is your daughter Ada Elaine. "My gosh", I said, "This is fantastic. She looks just like you."

I had not noticed the nurse leave the room but here she was again and now had a little bundle wrapped in a blue blanket. Grethel said, "And now, my dear William, I would like you to meet your son, William Thomas, Junior." I was overwhelmed. I knew tears were running down my cheeks as they were on Elaine's. I was just overwhelmed! I couldn't think of a word to say. I just stood there grinning foolishly at the two little bundles in my arms. The nurse came back in then with another little blue wrapped bundle and Grethel announced, "and here, William, is you other son, Three. You remember, do you not, when we thought we might start numbering them when we ran out of names, even numbers for girls and odd for boys? I was dumbfounded!

Grethel looked over at then nurse then and said, "Alice, is that all of them? The nurse laughed and said she thought she had found *most* of them but she would check again just to be sure. When she saw the expression on my face, Grethel burst out laughing and said for me not to worry, that was really all of them----she was *fairly* sure. It was just a little hard to keep track in all the excitement of the moment. She laughed some more. "And now, my dear William", she asked, "Do you have anything you want to say to your wife?

Elaine was now holding Ada Elaine while I had Three and William, Junior. I looked at Grethel a few moments and then said,* "Golly! I Was Sure You Knew; That I was Only Kidding! This wasn't at all necessary. I kept telling both of you, over and over again, *not numerous, humorous.* however, as long as we have gone to all this trouble I suppose we might just as well keep all of them. Grethel said not to worry, she would try and limit the number in the future. In any event, she was not planning to add any more to the family----at least for another *nine months* or so. When she saw the expression on my face, she burst out laughing again. I never will get in the last word, will I?

I told Grethel I had not expected her to be in such fine humor after all she must have gone through. She told me that actually all that was over with some time ago and yes, it was exhausting, very. She had not wanted me to see her when she looked like she had been dragged through a knothole backward. I might not let her have any more additions to the family if I had. She remembered however that I *had* used the word numerous and had heard it very clearly. She was confident she could live up to my stated expectations----with a little help from me------of course.

I said then, "Oh my gracious, my Dear, in all the excitement I forgot to mention I leave tomorrow, early, to return to Europe. There was an urgent matter there that needs my attention in Russia, or maybe it was Uzbekistan. I had forgotten the details but it was very important I get an early start. I'm sure it will come to me as soon as I get there. Grethel laughed gaily saying, "My Dear, Sweet, William, you won't be going anywhere for a long, long time, if ever. I might let you out of the house occasionally when I am satisfied you can be trusted to behave yourself and stay out of mischief. And, my dear William------don't think I am unaware that there was much that went on during your last little escapade that I have not—as yet, heard about. We shall no doubt discuss those interesting details more fully later on, when I have been restored to my full *strength* and *viguor*. (This is the weaker sex?)

Chapter Nine

Well, for almost a month, Grethel, Ada, Billy and Three have been home. Actually Three, I have learned, is named, Charles William. Grethel said she just could not resist playing that joke on me at the hospital. Elaine refers to him as "Prince Charlie," and he acts as if he believes this is his just due. Elaine has been here almost every day. Elke/Elvira has taken over some of her duties at the Roadrunner and she also comes over to help out when she can. Elaine just can't seem to keep her hands off Ada Elaine. I do suspect that this is going to be one spoiled little girl before long. Elaine has informed us that, as a Godmother, it is incumbent upon her to insure that each of her godchildren are not in need of anything and are all receiving the proper care.

I have now found out that both Grethel and Elaine have known for some time there was going to be more than just one addition to the family. They had decided they would have more fun with me if they kept that knowledge to themselves. I have asked them both if they thought this little oversight on their part was something that would soon pass from my mind. I have assured them both that my memory banks have been firmly imprinted with their chicanery. There will come a time, likely when they have long forgotten about this, and then *I* shall *wreak* my *vengence.* They have good cause to worry. They must, by now, be aware how *vicious* I can be when sufficiently ired. They both laughed merrily. Hah!

This place is a beehive of activity. Three tiny babies sure do require a lot of looking after. I suspect we are going to have to hire some help before long. We certainly can't expect Elaine, with a business to run, to be here every day from now on. It seems to me also that Grethel is beginning to look pretty tired. I don't remember when she has had a full night's sleep. I must confess the same thing also applies to me. Thank goodness, there are only three of them. Now that I know Grethel so well, it would not surprise me if she had decided to have her full quota, and I shudder to think what that might be, and probably all at one time.

I guess it is a good thing we did not find a house to buy right away. It is surprising how three such tiny people can make what I used to think as a fair sized house, seem quite crowded. Elaine has suggested I look around for a small hotel I might pick up at a good price. Very funny.

CHAPTER TEN

TWO WEEKS LATER, I got a phone call from the Major in the late morning. It was night in Twyford he said. He also went on to say the weather was abominable, cold and damp with a raw wind I told him I knew of a place with a much better climate and he said he surely hoped there was such a place somewhere. The reason he phoned was because he and Roberta were ready to get Gretchen out of Europe and to the US. My friends, the Bobs had made all the arrangements and Gretchen was cleared for permanent resident status. Gretchen was so happy she was beside herself he said. I told him that 'Elvira', her daughter, was using the name of Greenwood so likely they should use that for her passport and other documents as well. He agreed. As soon as he and Roberta had firmed up their plans, they would both be on the way and would contact me.

Ten days later I got a phone call from LA. A Mrs. Greenwood and her daughter had arrived from Ireland; would I accept a collect call? Of course! Roberta said they had arrived the day before. 'Mother' wanted to see Disneyland before they came up here. They would probably arrive by bus, as they wanted to see some of the countryside on the way. She would phone again when they knew their arrival time. I said we were all anxiously awaiting their arrival.

Grethel was so excited. It had been years since she had seen her aunt. A great many things had happened since then. When I told Elke her mother would be here before much longer she began crying. The last time she had seen her she had still been very ill and in the hospital. My extended family was growing by leaps and bounds. Maybe Elaine's idea of a small hotel was not so far-fetched after all. I wonder just how many more there are likely to be.

"Giselle' and her daughter, 'Roxanne', will be arriving on a tour bus. Roberta had discovered, with the help of their hotel concierge, that they could take a tour that started with a day at Disneyland. It would take two days then before they reached Bishop, where there tour would spend the night. They might leave the tour then unless 'Giselle' decided she wanted to continue on to Reno and then San Francisco. She had read so much about them. They would spend the first night at Victorville. They would arrive in the afternoon and would get to visit Roy and Dale Rogers museum in Apple Valley. They were assured they would likely meet the "King of the Cowboys" in person as he was often there and happy to greet visitors. There would also be stops in Cramer Junction, Little Lake and in Lone Pine, long enough to get a look at Mt. Whitney the highest point in the lower forty-eight. They were expecting to arrive at the Sierra Motor Lodge around three in the afternoon. Their lodging there was included in the tour price. They will phone after they have checked in.

Chapter Eleven

At four o'clock on the appointed day, Roberta phoned. They were all checked in, had showered, rested a bit and were now ready to receive visitors. I said we had been eagerly awaiting her call. I would be by in a trice to fetch them to our domicile. Roberta said they were waiting for me but just come in the car; she didn't know if both of them would fit into a trice. Sheeesh----try to inculcate a modicum of culture into people and see what you get. At least, she had the grace to giggle.

What a surprise! It was obvious that Gretchen had done much more than just *recover* from her accident. She was an entirely different looking person. I suspect that Roberta had been the one responsible for this dramatic change. What a smart looking middle-aged lady she appeared to be now. I told her how well she looked and she said, "Thank you, Wilhelm; it is so nice of you to notice." I said and not only that but her English was great as well. She said, Nien, no, Wilhelm. It is besser only. I practiced what to you I might haff to say. I told her, never mind, she was doing very well and she would get better every day she was here. I was sure the young men of our town were going to find her accent very sexy. She blushed and began stammering and Roberta told me to stop teasing and take us home.

Elke, Grethel and Elaine were waiting at home and I knew they would have the living room all decorated again with welcome home banners and other decorations. What a happy reunion it turned out to be. Elke and her mother ware overjoyed to be back together. Grethel was happy to see the aunt she had not had any contact with for so long.

Grethel, of course could not wait to show off the additions to the Thomas family. There they were, two pale blue bassinets with a pink one in between. I must confess, they were without a doubt, three of the handsomest babies to be seen anywhere in a long, long time. Of course, the babies had to be held. Elaine would consent to the holding of Three or William Junior but no one was allowed to hold Ada Elaine except Elaine herself. Little Ada must only be held in just a certain way.

Grethel and Elaine told them how they had kept the fact there were to be multiple births from me and then about the naming of Three. Everyone had a good laugh. It's a good thing I'm around or there would never be anything to inject a little humor into the da**y**'s activities. When I mentioned this, they laughed even harder. I told them then that there was a veritable host of ladies out there just waiting to get their hands on me who would show me the respect that a gentleman of my stature should expect and they laughed even harder, if that were possible. I told them then to beware, they could push me too far and that is when Gretchen came to my rescue and told them they should be nicer to Wilhelm who was really a very nice man. I told Gretchen, "Thank you" and what a nice lady *she* was. I hoped that when she was around here a while some of that "niceness" might transfer to some other ladies that I could point out if I were not, as she so aptly put it," *a nice* man".

Gretchen and Roberta were of course captivated by the babies, as everyone else had been. Roberta wanted to know if she could not have just one of them. No one needed to have three, she claimed. I told her I was inclined to agree with her but it was too early to figure out which one of the three we could spare.

I said I would take everyone to dinner at the club but we must have someone to watch over the babies while we were away. Grethel said, as their mother, she would take on that job. Elaine however said she was their Godmother and as such, this was the time that a godmother should take over. She would stay here while we went to dinner. Maybe we would bring her a crust of bread and a toothpick when we returned. She was used to suffering, as we all very well knew. Grethel finally agreed. We would have the cell phone and Elaine could reach us if there was an emergency. She even had Elaine dial the number from our home phone then to be sure it was going to work. Of course it did and we left for dinner.

Gretchen sat next to me at dinner. She wanted to talk and to thank me for getting them away from East Berlin. It was amazing to hear how dramatically her life had changed. She would be forever grateful. I told her I was truly glad she was happy in her new life. I told her it would be impossible for a champion "Sauerbraten Chef" to be left languishing in such unhappy circumstances. I hoped she and 'Elvira' were going to be very happy in this country. The both said that so far, living here had been unbelievable. Elvira explained to her mother about her new name and said she had decided to keep it. She went on to tell her mother of all things she had been doing since she had come here. Gretchen said she had been a skier when she was a girl and perhaps she could sometime go with Elvira. Elvira promised that would be soon. There was always equipment for rent at either Mammoth or June Lake.

Gretchen then asked if we would be unhappy if she continued with the rest of the tour, she had never had a vacation like this. She was having such a good time. Roberta said she would go with her. She also was having a good time and still had more of her thirty days leave to use. They should be back in a week. We all urged they go ahead with their plan. Roberta had never been to Reno either and had not been to San Francisco for a long time. She would enjoy seeing it again. They would be here for tomorrow in any event and we would have time for us all to get reacquainted before they continued the tour.

Chapter Twelve

GRETCHEN, OR GISELLE AS she is now to be called, has been back since yesterday. Her travelling companion, 'Roxanne' is here also. I think Roberta will just revert to her regular name for the time being. She phoned me and said we needed to talk. I said why don't we meet at the Sheriff place and she agreed. We did so, one hour later.

She asked to see the photos Alf had taken and I had them in the desk I used whenever Verne decided I should *volunteer*. Roberta said she had not wanted to alarm anyone without just cause but she had observed two men on a couple occasions that appeared to be watching them too closely, one time in Reno and again in San Francisco. There was something about them that just did not seem right to her. She had said nothing to Gretchen about this because she did not wish to alarm her unnecessarily when it could be possible she was mistaken.

Most of the time of course they had been with the rest of their tour group. I had phoned my friend Jim, at the Post Office in Reno and he had taken them to dinner the only night they had free there. Their only free time in San Francisco had been spent with Al.

After examining the photos, she thought one of those was one of the two men but not the other. I asked her then if she could describe the other man and she did so. This is the sort of thing, which routinely, most agents could do very well. As she described in detail what she had seen I began to have a sinking feeling. I told her I thought she was describing Bruno Hauptmann. I was sorry there was no photo to show her. She suggested I pass my suspicions on to Al as soon as possible. His office said he would get back to me when he got back in town. What a revolting development this is! I thought we had gotten rid of this problem, once and for all.

When I told Verne about our new problem, he suggested I go back on the job. In uniform, I would have an excuse to be wearing a gun again. I would be happy to know my pay would stay at the same level as before. I said I agreed that might be a good idea. I was also glad that there had been no recent reduction in salaries. I didn't mention it but I was also going to be wearing my Kevlar underwear, the top anyway. I suspect, if they made jockeys of the same material, they could be just a tad scratchy. All the deputies were alerted to recheck the photos they had of the two suspects and to be aware there could be a third man with either or both of them. I sure hoped that I was mistaken in my suspicions, Bruno, I was sure, was a very dangerous man.

Al had not seen the photos Alf had taken so I made copies and faxed them to him with a cover letter. I did the same for Jim in Reno and to my friend, Deputy Ron Miller in Gardnerville. He might alert the Sheriff's Office up there. If I turn out to be wrong about this, I sure am going to look stupid. Everyone will think I am some kind of paranoid kook.

It was two days before I heard from Al. He had been having just a lovely time the past couple days attending meetings in DC, The seat of all power. It had been a real drag. He knew about Bruno from the letters we had intercepted in Reno and the lists Roberta and I had retrieved in Switzerland. He thought it possible there might be a picture of some kind in Bruno's file in Washington. He would have a check made. If so he would have it faxed to me at the Sheriff's office.

It appears Bruno has been a little shy about being photographed. The only picture they had was not very good. I could however recognize it as being Bruno. When I showed the faxed photo to Roberta, she said she was pretty sure that it was the second of the two men she had seen and she was sure now they had indeed been watching them. She said it was now time perhaps for Gretchen to really become someone different; perhaps to change her appearance even more. I wondered if we could do that without telling anyone why, at least until we were sure the danger was more imminent than it appeared to be at the moment.

Roberta said it would be a cinch. Gretchen was already intending to embark on a totally new life. She would be convinced that this makeover was a part of doing just that. She would see to it immediately. Also, she said, it was better she and daughter, Elvira not live together for now. If these people were looking for a mother-daughter combination, they must be sure not to give that impression in any way. Roberta said she would hang around a few more days. She and Giselle would continue to room together at the hotel. We should have more information in a few more days on which to make any further plans.

Grethel, Elaine and Elvira wondered why I was wearing all my Deputy stuff again all of a sudden. I told them Verne was now unexpectedly short-handed. I had agreed to help him out for a while. That seemed to satisfy everyone and I went into the office every day for a short time to maintain this façade. What I had not expected was to actually be put to work. Criminee! Gretchen, 'Giselle', had never seen me all decked out in my Deputy stuff and was quite impressed with me. Girls *do* seem to like a man in uniform don't they. The ladies all told me I was very impressive in my nice "Deputy Suit". A curse I will just have to live with I expect.

Chapter Thirteen

I AM NOT A superbly trained investigator for nothing. Something is going on. I can't put my finger on just what it is but I will find out before long. I have been at the office a lot lately and Giselle has been helping Grethel quite a bit of the time. All the other ladies seem to be hanging around the house more than normal. They are all giving me that 'funny' look on occasion. I know Grethel can't be expecting agin; she wouldn't dare. However, something is up for sure. One thing I have noticed that with Giselle's help, Grethel has been looking a lot more rested lately.

Giselle has decreed that it is now time Grethel should get out of the house for a change of scenery. She will assume supervision of the young Thomas's. I have been designated to take her out for a nice lunch. Well, that is certainly something I can manage. It has also been determined that I am to meet her at the Roadrunner at eleven-thirty, *precisely*. That is also something I can manage. Tomorrow it is, rain or shine. OK, I shall be there with bells on, hair slicked and shoes shined.

And, there I was, walking through the entrance to the Roadrunner at precisely eleven-thirty. The hostess told me my party was waiting for me and to please come with her. She led me to a large table over in the corner. Grethel stood up immediately and said, "Welcome to the first annual meeting of the William's Wives Club, my dear William." Also at the table were Elaine, Roberta and Elvira. "We are just about to have the champagne poured", she continued, "Why don't you just sit here next to me, the head wife." I have a sneaking feeling that I may be in for a bad time. I did notice however that everyone was smiling.

Grethel continued: "You may remember, my dear that I had mentioned to you that I was aware that I had not gotten the full story about your escapades while you were running around all over Europe. I also mentioned that, you may recall, when I had regained my strength that lack of information from you would be corrected. I knew of course that *you* would never tell me all the details I wanted to know therefore-----after applying sufficient pressure, I was able to get a *full* account from both Roberta and Elvira. It took some time but I finally heard *everything*, even the part where you tried to wear your shoes and socks in bed with Elvira. I think we may make a short movie of that. if I can find someone to play your part.

Roberta and Elvira finally told me of course why and how they acted the part of your wife, what a good boy you actually had been and how they had teased you. That is how we came up with the name for our little club. Elaine of course has not had to act as your wife in any capacity---at least that I have as yet been able to ascertain. However, she *is* the Godmother of the first installment of your *numerous* offspring so we have voted to name her an honorary member. We likely will have an annual meeting again sometime next year. It is my sincere hope that it will not have become necessary to add to the membership list before that event occurs. And now, my dear William", she concluded. "Do *you* have any comments you wish to make? I said, "My dear, Grethel, I know that if I were to say anything at all it would likely only make my situation worse. If you don't mind, I think I will just sit here quietly and eat my lunch."

Grethel leaned over, gave me a kiss, and said she knew I had not told her all the things that had happened because I thought it would have upset her. She wanted me to know that she was *very* proud of me and of all that I had accomplished. Please, *just do not do it anymore.* My numerous offspring needed to have a father around to assist in their proper upbringing. After that, we had a nice lunch and Roberta and Elvira added to some of the stories they had told Grethel. I kept my mouth shut unless asked a direct question.

CHAPTER FOURTEEN

Elvira has already taken her mother skiing three times. She says that Giselle is actually quite good. They usually go on a Monday. It is less crowded that day and the restaurant is also closed and Elvira is not needed there to keep all the young bachelors in town happy and coming in for lunch. Elvira says that her mother, in her new makeover, is sure attracting some attention on the slopes from some of the men. Laughing, she says she is wondering now if she needs this competition. She is actually very pleased that her mother is getting on so well in her new life after the grim times she had gone through for so long back in East Berlin.

This Monday Roberta has gone with them. She also skis quite well I have been told. I guess that should not be a surprise, that lady seems to be able to do almost anything and do it well. There is just supposed to be light snow flurries in the higher elevations so they should have a good time. I helped Grethel get the offspring all situated and everything pretty much in order and went off to the Sheriff's office. I told Grethel I would check with her around noon to see if she needed anything.

It was a kind of ho-hum morning. I phoned home about twelve-thirty and was informed everything was fine. Three had been a little bit fussy earlier but he was fine now. She calls him that whenever she thinks she can get a rise out of me. A little after one, I got a phone call. I should have known this peace and quiet was too good to last. The call was from Oscar Mason, a Deputy in the Mono County Sheriff's office I had met some time previously. He was phoning from their sub-station in Mammoth.

It appeared that Gretchen, 'Giselle', and her daughter had been kidnapped from the slopes while skiing this morning. It had been snowing at the time but not heavily. Elvira, who had been farther up the slope at the time, thought she saw the two men who had taken them, although through the snow, she had not realized what was happening until it was too late to get help. I told Oscar that no matter what happened, not to let Elvira out of his sight at any time until I could get there. I would be there as soon as I could. I left word for Verne describing what had happened.

I phoned Grethel next and told her what had occurred and I couldn't spend any time talking. I must be on my way at once. She told me she understood and to be careful. I phoned Elaine on my cell phone when I was underway and told her what had happened and asked, if she could get away, to go to Grethel and also try and get word to Al as soon as possible. Be sure all the doors and windows are locked at home and be on the lookout for any strangers. She said she was on her way at once and would call Al from my house.

I made it to Mammoth in fifty minutes. It was snowing a little heavier now. As soon as I stepped into the office Elvira flew into my arm, weeping. She was sure everything was her fault although Oscar kept assuring her there was nothing else she could have done. She had notified them immediately, which was the right thing to do. I told her with the weather worsening this way, I was sure they could not get far. We would catch up to them soon. Oscar said they had already put out road blocks; there are only a couple ways in an out and they had them covered. As soon as the weather cleared, they would have the helicopter up also. He had gotten copies of the pictures of our suspects and they had been distributed to all the deputies.

It was obvious Roberta had been mistaken for Elvira. Wearing a hat and snow goggles, as she was, that would be easy to do. They were both about the same size and it was quite possible the kidnappers did not even know they had the wrong person. We waited at the command post that had been set up by the ski .lifts, all of which were now closed.

Before long, I got a phone call from Gil Montoya, the Sheriff of Mono County. He reminded me they had made me an honorary deputy some time ago. He was counting on me to help them out now. Right, we were waiting reports to come in from the deputies out in the field. It was snowing harder now. Criminee! I'm sure I must be getting too old for this sort of thing all the time. I'm afraid I'm not up to the challenge anymore. I really want to get out of here and go home.

CHAPTER FIFTEEN

W<small>E HAD BEEN STANDING</small> around for a couple hours. Nothing but negative reports were coming in from the road blocks. At four, Elaine called me. A phone call for me had come at the house. It was from Bruno Hauptmann; at least that is whom he said he was when Grethel had answered. When she had said that yes, she was Mrs. Thomas, he said she was to tell Herr Thomas, "we have Frau Gretchen and fraulein, Elke in a safe place". He would contact Herr Thomas again with certain instructions when he determined the time was right for him to do so. Then, "do please to take good care of the little Kinder, Mrs. Thomas. It would be a shame if anything bad should happen to them."

Grethel was terrified and so distraught she could not call me. I told Elaine I would be home in about an hour. Verne should be back at the office. Phone him and fill him in on what has happened. Tell Grethel I will take care of everything. I told Oscar what had happened and he agreed, I had better be on my way. We would keep in touch. I told him I would phone him when I reached home. I made it in fifty-five minutes and made the call from the cell phone in my car. He had nothing further to report.

Chapter Sixteen

As soon as I got inside Grethel clung to me. When she could finally speak she said, "Oh, William, I am so frightened. I haven't been so afraid since those two men grabbed me in Wiesbaden. I never thought to have to go through this again. If anything should happen to the children, I fear I will lose my mind." I told her she must be calm. We could not cope with this situation if we did not keep our heads. I told her there was no way those people could get to the children. Part of their plan is to have us upset and confused. We must not allow that to happen. I pointed out that she had coped with danger before. I said I had every confidence that she would handle this as she had done in the past.

Elaine had been standing by listening to this. I could tell she was just as upset as Grethel at the thought of anything happening to her godchildren, especially to little Ada Elaine. Then she said, "Bill is right, Greth," it is up to us to keep our wits about us. You know that Bill is not going to let harm come to any of us." She came over then so I could include her in all the hugging that was going on. I called Oscar back then and gave him the house phone number and said that all was OK here. He said he figured I would have everything under control and was sending Elvira home with a deputy. There would be a Deputy following as backup and the deputy driving Elvira would ride back to Mammoth with him. I thanked him and told him I would keep him up to date on anything developing here. He gave me his cell phone number to pass on to Verne. Whoever it was that developed these cell phones sure does deserve a medal. Too bad they are so bulky.

Elaine said then that she had started a big pot of coffee when they knew I was coming home and that was ready. Why didn't we sit down, have some coffee and gather our thoughts. She had phoned Verne as I had asked and he would be by before long to check thing out here. She had no sooner finished telling us that than we heard a car pulling up and there was Verne. He was glad to share some coffee with us, as he hadn't had anything since breakfast. As soon as she heard that Grethel jumped up and had sandwich stuff out and one made before he had time to say it was too much trouble.

We were all sitting around the kitchen table now. Verne said they had been trying to trace the call Grethel had gotten but .likely it would turn out to be from a cell phone. I said if that were so and they could find the frequency, it might be possible to intercept future transmissions and perhaps get some valuable information on the kidnappers. He remembered now, that was how those guys with the helicopter had found Grethel and me. He phoned the office immediately and had them start on that right away. All deputies had been alerted on what had happened today and were to be on the lookout for the two men whose photos they had been given.

We decided that Elvira, 'Elke', would stay here. Elaine said she would stay as well. I still had those extra bedrooms I had not, as yet, filled with the additional Thomasrs that I had promised and they would use those. Verne said, probably a good idea having everyone in one place. It would be much easier to provide protection that way. He had talked to Al in San Francisco who reminded him that kidnapping was a federal offence and the FBI would likely soon be involved. Agents would likely be here soon especially as this was all tied in with the escape network. Al had also notified the CIA in DC that one of their agents had been kidnapped. I do believe we are going to be pretty busy around here very soon. .

Forty-five minutes later Elvira was at the door with two Mono County deputies. They didn't seem to have minded at all guarding Elvira. They however had to refuse the offer of coffee as they were due back in Mammoth as soon as they could make it. Things were pretty busy up there. They were going to start a house-to-house search, which was going to take some time. All available personnel were needed. Right now, a car with bullhorn was patrolling the streets announcing the kidnapping of two women by two or three men and that a house-to-house search was soon to be underway. No one would be allowed into or out of Mammoth until that had been completed. I told them what a fine job they were doing and they left to return to their jobs.

Elvira was so upset about her mother. She had only recently

recovered from her terrible ordeal with the car wreck in England, now this! Grethel and Elaine had been hugging and petting her and trying to console her. Grethel said, "You know, Elvira, William was able to rescue both of you in Berlin. I am certain he will be able to do the same for your mother and Roberta. Golly! And here I am, with not the faintest idea of what to do next. I hope they don't discover they have Roberta instead of Elke. If Bruno is around here somewhere and the kidnapper are in Mammoth they might not discover their mistake for a while. Bruno is the only one who knows what Elke looks like. With her dark hair, "Elvira" now looks much different. Roberta on the other hand really *is* a blond.

There will be Deputies watching, once our lights go out, until morning. As soon as everyone has gone to bed, I will activate the alarm system. I warned everyone not to wander around during the night or there were going to be unpleasant surprises. I didn't think my old heart could stand too many more of them.

Now listen all, I told them. I would turn the system off at six thirty in the morning. I would then expect all of them to line up for roll call and inspection. At that time, I would issue any orders of the day and make any assignments I thought appropriate. I said all of this with a perfectly straight face. For a few minutes, there was total silence as they stood around jaws hanging open. Then I said, "Very well, if there are no questions you may all now retire to your quarters. I shall blow my whistle at six-thirty tomorrow morning and you will then have fifteen minutes to appear and line up for roll-call and inspection." That's when they all pounced on me, laughing and giggling. Well, it did lighten the mood and everyone was now laughing and joking, about me and my *funny* ideas, as they went off to bed.

CHAPTER SEVENTEEN

I HAD SUGGESTED WE get breakfast under way early. I was pretty sure we would have visitors quite early. Also, let's have extra coffee available. As soon as I got up, I went to the bakery and got four dozen assorted hot, fresh, doughnuts. As I plunked them down by the coffee urn, I told the ladies they were not allowed to have any. It would spoil their breakfast and besides that, they were *very, very,* fattening. As usual, they didn't heed one word of what I said. I guess I was lucky I was allowed one for myself.

The first contingent arrived at seven fifteen, Al and another agent along with Verne. Al had left two other agents at Mammoth the night before. They all decided that if doughnuts and coffee were going to be here every day this was going to be their first stop in the morning. Al told us the FBI was also trying to trace the call Grethel had gotten from Bruno.

Verne had been talking to the Mono County Sheriff's office and they said they had a blanket over all of Mammoth. They swore even a gnat could not get out without being spotted. Now we have to hope the kidnappers had not gotten out before everything was bottled up. I think our best bet would be to spot their cell phone channel and perhaps get a clue to where they were hiding out. Al says that scanners are working full time and the phone company has also been alerted. Now I guess we can only wait and hope there is another call from Bruno before long.

During the day, I have been keeping a close watch. Bruno or one of his henchmen might try to find out what we are doing. So far, I have not seen one thing that looked suspicious. The night-watchers reported that they had seen no one loitering around anywhere near us. Our street normally has cars passing by all day and sometimes in the evening but seldom late at night. Of course, someone could just drive on by and not be noticed.

A car did drive up to our house about eleven forty-five. Two men, wearing outdoor clothes, as if they might have been up in the mountains, came to the door. Boy was I glad to see them! It was my favorite Bobs, next to Roberta of course; Berlin Bob and Prague Bob. Neither had had time to eat since early this morning and when I mentioned there was still some hot coffee and some doughnuts we had two quite happy campers.

Elaine had put on a fresh pot of coffee and we all sat around the table to wait for it to finish brewing. I said the wait would be worth it. That old coffee in the urn had been sitting there for some time and to say it was getting a tad strong would be a considerable understatement. I introduced Grethel and Elaine then. Berlin Bob turned out to be Timothy O'Callaghan and Prague Bob was Robert Waggoner." Remember Deputy", he reminded me, I told you, I was the only real Bob in the bunch." They were pleased to meat Grethel whom they had heard so much about. They couldn't get over how much she and Elvira, who they knew of course as Elke, looked so much alike. I said they should have seen Elvira when she was a blond. The resemblance then was really startling. They said they had already talked to Agent Clarke and he had carefully instructed them to note the ring Elaine was wearing; it was the one he had given her when they *had become engaged*; don't bother getting any ideas. Elaine was pleased to show off her ring and when asked verified, yes, she was very much engaged to Agent Clarke.

Tim told us that "The Company" took a very dim view of anyone who sought to harm any of their people. That is why they had been sent to give us any help they could in the rescue of Roberta. They had been brought up to date on all that had happened and like the rest of us were now waiting for further contact from the kidnappers or for the team at Mammoth to find something. In the meantime, they had come to see me; they knew I would be upset if they did not at least pay a call at the clubhouse. I showed them the plaque then that was hanging in the den and told them when we built our house it would have a much more suitable housing. I promised that a revisit at that time would be well worth their while.

Well it was late now. The coffee and doughnuts were all gone. The Bobs had my phone number now and they gave me their phone number at the motel plus their cell phone numbers. I gave them my cell phone number also and would have that phone with me if I left the house. For now, I guess I am the resident guard—except for the doughnut run early in the morning. They left after Grethel had them inspect the first installment of "William's *numerous* children." Boy, I sure am going to have some reputation with the Bobs. Gosh, do you remember, it seems like only a few weeks ago, that I left my home down south to spend just a few days visiting my old stamping grounds up in the Sierras? Unbelievable!

Chapter Eighteen

IT WAS ANOTHER DAY before we heard from Bruno again. We had decided that either Elaine or Grethel would answer any calls. I was afraid that Bruno might recognize Elvira's voice. We were still hoping he had not yet discovered they had the wrong person for Gretchen's daughter. Any caller that asked for me would be told that I was out in the garage and they would call me to the phone in just a minute. That might give us time to trace the call frequency, we hoped.

Luckily, Verne and Al were with us having coffee when the call did come in. When the caller had asked for me, they immediately got on their cell phones and the people on the scanners and at the phone company were alerted.

I couldn't wait too long in answering. Bruno might get suspicious and hang up. When I said, "Hello, Bruno, I never expected to hear from you again after we said good bye in Berlin" , he chuckled; "Ah my so clever freund, Herr Thomas. You remember. I told you I expected to see you in California. You are perhaps not so clever as you might have hoped. I must confess however that you und your freunds have caused me und mine freunds much inconvenience. You are now going to be required to pay back for all the trouble you have caused for us.

You have, now for us, unfortunately rendered the US and especially your California, unsuitable for us to continue here our operations. We must shift to Mexico our operations and that costs money. You, mine dear Herr Thomas, are to us now going to be of assistance. Oh, I know you are trying to trace this call but your time you will waste. In my little auto, I am driving about and using one of the cellular telephones you seem to so many of in this country have. You can never where I now am, locate. As you can see, mine dear Herr Thomas, you are not the only clever one.

You have money that to us rightly belongs. We now want that

back, plus interest. It is important for the health and safety of Frau Groenwald and Fraulein Elke that you have for us the one hundred and fifty thousand dollars that you now are owing to us. This you must be doing without delay. I will again phone you from somewhere, tomorrow or the day after, at a time that is to me convenient, with for you, further instructions. Auf Weidersehn, Herr Thomas.----Click.

Well, we know now that Bruno is not with the men that did the kidnapping. They must still be bottled up somewhere in the mountains. It has been a few days and about now and they possibly could be getting a little nervous. If they were to become aware they had a Central Intelligence Agent instead of Elke, they likely would be having fits. If they *did* make that discovery, they might also decide she was too dangerous to remain alive. If we are going to do anything, I think we must do it soon.

Verne and Al had been busy on the phones, trying to see if anyone of the scanners had picked up the cell phone frequency. Twenty minutes later, they had the word; one of the scanners had picked up the frequency and had actually heard the last few seconds of Bruno's conversation. Now let us hope he tries to phone his confederates and that they let slip some clue that will let us figure out where they are holed up. I got one of the scanners then so I also could listen at home. They also had one tuned in to the frequency at Mammoth and another at the Sheriff's office both of which would be manned twenty-four hours a day. OK, come on you guys, somebody make a call so we can grab you.

It gets dark early this time of year. It was just getting dusk when a call came in on the kidnapper's frequency. Someone was very excited and jabbering away in German. I grabbed Elke and Grethel, gave them pencils and paper, and asked they translate what they could. I thought I heard Bruno's voice trying to interrupt the tirade but without success. Abruptly the transmission ceased. Elke and Grethel had been writing furiously trying to get down as much as possible of what they had heard. Finally, they looked up. They were ready.

I can't help it. I'm sorry but this reminds me of the days when we were kids. On Saturdays we would take our dimes and go to the matinee at the Avalon Theatre. In addition to the movie, usually a Western and the cartoon, there was the serial movie. This always stopped just as everyone was holding their breath at the most exciting moment. Now you had to be back the next Saturday for the next episode. Ya wanna get a root beer or cup of coffee now? OK. OK., here we go.

CHAPTER NINETEEN

Y OU NEEDN'T GET TESTY. Elvira took down what she heard in German while Grethel translated what she could into English. Between them they had pretty much gotten the gist of the harangue we had heard. It was pretty much a one-sided conversation with the kidnappers doing most of the talking as Bruno tried to interrupt them.

They had been holed up with their captives in this out of the way cabin that Bruno had found in Mammoth. They had heard the loudspeakers of the deputies and were aware of the search that was underway. They knew when the house-to-house search was started and they knew that the searchers would soon reach them.

It had been snowing off and on and last night. While it was snowing heavily, they had stolen two snowmobiles. They had not driven anything like this before but eventually got things underway and had left a little before dawn with their hostages tied on behind them. They believed they had gotten away undetected. Being unfamiliar with the operations of these machines and with the women tied on behind it was slow going. Not having the right clothing, they were almost frozen stiff and ready to kill off the hostages. They thought all of this a stupid waste of time.

They had headed south generally following near the highway they figured must lead to where Bruno must be hiding out. Not long after leaving Mammoth, they had crossed a road leading to a place having something to do with convicts. They thought it was too close to where they had just left and were also uncertain as to what the name might mean. It could lead to some kind of prison camp and they decided it best to go on.

They were not making very good time and knew they must soon find a place to hide out before it got too light. Before long they had come in sight of what looked like a little crossroads settlement and a narrow, snow covered road there led up into the mountains. They had taken that road. There had been no tracks in the snow and they were hoping the new snow would soon cover any tracks *they* made.

A half hour later they thought they could see buildings a couple hundred yards to their left and deciding to take a chance, had proceeded there. They crossed a small bridge and it appeared this was a camp of some kind closed up for the winter. They had broken into one of the building and had dragged enough wood inside to help them thaw out their frozen bodies. They had no sooner gotten the wood over to the cabin when one of the snow machines stopped. Likely they were out of gasoline.

They had been able to start a fire and thawed out a little but they had no food. They had left the hostages tied up in one of the rooms and were then so exhausted they had fallen asleep. They then took turns searching the camp for something to eat. All they could find after hours of searching were two cans of frozen beans and one small can of frozen pineapple, none of which they could open. The temperature must be way below freezing. They did not have the proper footwear and their feet were now very painful. FIND THEM AND GET THEM OUT OF HERE----- NOW!

I bet I know where they are!

Verne phoned; I figured he would. He had heard the transmission at the Sheriff's station but of course, no one understood German. I told him both Grethel and Elvira had listened and I thought I knew where the kidnappers were. I also said I thought we had better get there without delay. We would need something to negotiate the heavy snow we would likely encounter. He would get their winterized jeep he said and would pick me up very soon.

I had Grethel and Elvira making coffee and sandwiches and by the time Verne arrived, that was all packed up and we were ready to go. By now, I had on my snow boots and all my cold weather gear. Verne was similarly attired. As we started out, I told Verne where I thought we would find our kidnappers. He knew of the place but had not been there in some time. The county line was just a short way above the camp and he never had much reason to go there. I sure hope I hadn't miscalculated and the kidnappers were somewhere else.

When we turned off the highway at Tom's Place, it became slow going. The oversize snow tires however kept us moving ahead and a half hour or so later I told Verne this was the place to let me out. The road leading over to the lodge was just ahead. I would cut through the woods to the bridge and I was pretty sure I could get into the camp without been noticed. He would continue on about six hundred yards and he would see another road. It leads to the far end of the camp and the lower corral of the pack station. Verne had been driving without lights for the last ten minutes but with all the new white snow, it was really quite light from the bright starlight. I just hope the snow under the trees is not too deep. From here, it is only a couple hundred yards to the bridge; the camp's buildings, I knew, were not far beyond that.

I couldn't resist. As I got out of the jeep, I said to Verne, "I sure hope you remembered to bring a gun, Verne. In all the excitement, I forgot mine. You should have seen the look of dismay on his face. He finally realized I had been kidding him and with a snort, drove on and left me. He will reach the other access road in a few minutes. There are trees on both sides of that one, almost down to the river. He can leave the jeep in the road where the trees end. Verne will start at the upper end of the camp and I at the lower and try to locate the cabin of the kidnappers as we work toward each other. The camp is heavily wooded and we should be able to move about unseen if we are careful.

Trudging through two feet of snow in the woods at this altitude gets to you pretty soon. I hadn't realized how tough this was going to be. I should have let Verne out here and taken the other end; that is easier going. Verne could likely have handled this end better; he is younger and probably in better condition besides. I finally made it down to the bridge by the creek and stopped to catch my breath. I didn't see a soul. It was quiet as a tomb except for a little gurgle from the almost solidly frozen stream. I crouched down and slipped across the bridge in seconds. I was sure no one had seen me. There was no sign of life and not a glimmer of light to be seen anywhere. You would think they would have a light of some kind if they were here. Maybe Verne is having better luck at his end; he should be there by now.

There were only scattered snowflakes coming down now. I had looked for tracks of a snowmobile but had seen nothing. They could be covered by snow by now of course. I was beginning to think this had all been a big mistake when, aha----I smelled wood smoke. As old Brigham had once said, "This must be the place." Of course, there was no light because they didn't have any. These cabins, I knew had all had a kerosene lamp for emergencies in the old days. But it is not .likely they would know to look for one, assuming the cabins still have them..

Golly Ned! It was colder than a gravedigger's nose. If I hadn't worn my heavy snow boots and my insulated parka I would have been frozen solid. I followed my nose and before long found the cabin. It was one of the cabins I had used from time to time some years back. There was a kitchen, all-purpose room in the middle and sleeping rooms on each end. The stove for this one I knew was near the back wall of the main room. I suppose they might all be in that room near the stove.

And, sure enough, there were the snowmobiles. They were so covered by snow I hadn't seen them at first. I couldn't hear a sound from inside. Now to find Verne. Keeping to the shadows, I worked toward the other end of the grounds and then spotted Verne, crossing the bridge. I was beginning to fear he had missed the turn off and wound up at the lake. He had gotten stuck after I had left and it took him fifteen minutes to get the jeep extricated. He pointed out where he had left it back at the edge of the trees. I told him then what I had found.

It was so cold and deathly quiet that even whispers sounded like someone shouting. Sounds seemed magnified one hundred fold. We were creeping up to the cabin keeping out of sight of the big front window. It is dark inside so we can't see any of them but if they are looking out they would be able to see us. The starlight on the snow actually made it fairly bright except in the deep shadows where we crouched. We were near the back wall near one end when we heard the faint sound of women's voices. Then a man's voice barked something from another room and again all was quiet.. Well we know now that the women seem to be in the end room while the kidnappers were near the stove in the main room.

I beckoned to Verne and we moved far enough away that we could whisper without being heard in the cabin. I had an idea and when I explained, Verne whispered, "Let's do it". He couldn't think of anything better and time was a-wasting. I searched around under the trees and found a pinecone of the right size. I made my way as silently as a ghost to the back wall of the cabin. It was as I remembered. The stove pipe ran straight back through the wall and then had an elbow and went up past the eaves.

Let's hope they didn't fasten the joints together with sheet metal screws. That would be a problem. They pulled the pipes apart every spring when they reopened and cleaned out the pipes as I remembered so I don't expect they used permanent fastenings. And yes, it was as I thought. A sugar pine cone is just about the right diameter to plug up the four-inch pipe. It seemed to take forever to loosen the pipe at the elbow, trying to make as little noise a possible. What little noise there was, was covered by the noise of the fire in the stove. Now let's hope this works. I had shoved the cone into the pipe as far as it would go. If this works, we should get some action pretty soon.

Before long, we heard sounds. You did not have to be an expert in linguistics to know someone was cursing in German. Then we could hear banging on the stove. A lot of good that is going to do them. I went around to the end of the cabin opposite from Verne and gave him the high sign. We should get some action pretty soon if this is going to work at all. Verne and I each had our guns ready now. I moved about fifteen feet out from the building. We don't want to wind up shooting at each other from opposite ends of the cabin. I had mentioned to Verne earlier that I wouldn't be surprised if they didn't shove one of the women outside first to see what might happen.

Yep. that's what they did; the door flew open and a cloud of smoke gushed out and in the cloud was a person. The door was immediately shut except for a crack someone inside was trying to see through. We could see now that it was one of the women. Whoever it was had all their ski clothes on with snow hat and goggles. That might have helped a little with the smoke.

Whoever it was, hesitated a moment and then began walking straight ahead. I had seen Roberta walk often enough to recognize that it was she. As she came abreast of where I was I whispered, "Don't look, keep on walking and a little faster if possible." Verne saw what I had done so knew one of the hostages was now freed. Now, what are the kidnappers going to do when nothing happens to the first hostage and they cannot see anyone else around? Meanwhile more smoke was coming through the partly open door. I hope they do something soon or the fire will be going out and the smoke will stop. Right now it must be pretty thick.

Well I guess we aren't dealing with rocket scientist here. They pushed Gretchen out and I could see two faces at the front window as they tried to see what happened. Good old Roberta; she saw what had happened and called to Gretchen to keep on walking toward her. Soon they were both out of sight and I melted back into the shadows and made my way to them. Verne joined us a few minutes later; no sound at all from the kidnappers. Roberta said she didn't think they understood more than a few words of English.

Gretchen said that was true. She of course could understand all they said although she did not let on she understood them. They were very confused and frightened. They were also very cold and hungry. Roberta and Gretchen had on their warm ski clothes, the kidnappers were not so lucky; if they couldn't keep a fire going they would very soon suffer from Hypothermia. They had sweaters and overcoats but they were not enough and their shoes were totally inadequate. It was likely they could already be suffering frostbite.

I asked, "Do you think you ladies could handle a little hot coffee and maybe a sandwich about now?" Roberta said if she didn't know I was already married she would have married me right then. Gretchen said they had not had anything to eat for some time and only a little melted snow for water. I suggested to Verne that, while I kept an eye on things here, why not take the ladies to the jeep for some refreshments. Also he might just as well bring the jeep across and into the camp. It would still be out of sight of the cabin. The ladies could wait in the jeep then where it would be a little warmer. The ladies needed no urging and I soon saw them all hurrying across the bridge to find the jeep.

I moved back where I could have a good view of the cabin. Our would-be kidnappers must be sweating bullets about now. They don't know yet there is anyone else out here. Their hostages have however now disappeared from sight. Now they are probably worried what Bruno is going to do when he finds they have misplaced his hostages. I can see two faces peering out the front window. Every so often one face disappears; no doubt looking out the other widows. There is a lot of coughing going on. Half an hour later, I could see the jeep creeping through the trees. The lights were off and it stopped back a ways out of sight of the cabin.

Except for the coughing, there was no sound from the cabin so it was time I went back to get a closer look. First, however I was offered a little hot coffee which surely did hit the spot. I declined a sandwich for now. Roberta asked if we had any extra guns an I gave her my hide-out. Verne pointed out the shotgun in the rack in the jeep and Roberta said she could handle that too or most anything else we might have available. I said I knew from experience that was surely true; I had seen her in operation. Verne said then we better get back to the cabin, if the kidnappers did not come out and surrender soon we must try to encourage them to do so. The ladies could keep the jeep warm. Just leave the windows open a crack so it didn't get so fogged up they couldn't see.

By now, those two in the cabin must almost be basket cases. They haven't heard a sound and there is now no sign of their former hostages. The fire in their stove is out now and it must be getting colder. Verne said we would give them another half hour. In the meantime, he had used his cell phone and called headquarters to tell them the hostages were now safe. Most likely we would take the kidnappers prisoners before long. Alert the helicopter crews be ready for his call.

OK. The half hour is up. Verne had his bullhorn set at maximum volume. We had moved up close to the cabin now. He handed the horn to me and said, "OK, say something to get them moving." I picked up a rock, banged it hard against the side of the cabin a couple times and shouted into the bullhorn, "Rouse, rouse, rouse; Politzie, Politzie; machen zie schnell, schnell. Rouse, rouse, **rouse**!" Well, if they haven't had a heart attack I suspect they could now use a change of undergarments for sure. I propped my flashlight in a tree branch aimed at the window, turned it on and got out of the way. If someone decided that made a good target I didn't want to be standing next to it.

In just a few minutes, someone was waving a white rag in the window and then the door slowly opened. Someone was shouting, Komerad, Komerad. I guess we did it. I picked up the bullhorn and again and shouted, "rouse, rouse! Two of the most miserable and sorriest looking specimens came outside, hands raised. They were shivering both with fear and the cold. While Verne covered them, I went up and patted them down. They must have left their guns inside.

I went around the back then, removed the pinecone and shoved the pipes back together. We could start the fire again. Verne motioned for them to carry the rest of the wood inside and start the fire. Good thing someone had left old newspapers in the wood box. While they did this, I took my flashlight and found the kerosene lamp on the back of one of the closet shelves. I knew there had to be one in here somewhere. Verne had already confiscated the guns they had abandoned. There wasn't a lot of kerosene left in the lamp but it would do for tonight. With the lamp lit and the fire going things looked a lot better. Verne had put plastic restraints on the prisoners. They seemed to be happy to be thawing out. We sat them both at the kitchen table. Talk about dejected looks. They knew they were in for a really bad time. I didn't know enough German to talk to them and was about to suggest we call Gretchen in when a voice from the door said,

"Ah, mine goot freund, Herr Thomas, so we meet at last again. I see you have a freund with you. And, what have you done to mine goot Komerades? There stood good old Bruno with a small machine pistol pointed at my head. He must have known I would be wearing my bulletproof underwear. Where in the hell had he come from? "Again you have caused me much inconvenience", he said. "Now do not even twitch. Drop your guns on the floor." We had no choice but to obey. My head is hard but it is not bulletproof.

He said something to the kidnappers and they sat back down with smug looks on their faces. He hadn't cut them loose yet however. Now he continued. "I know you think you are very clever, Herr Thomas but there are others equally as clever. I had hoped we could be freunds when in Berlin we met but I know now that will never be possible. My Komerades and I have been here a little while now and I have been studying this part of California with the help of the so very good maps of your automobile club. That let me determine the location of mine Komerades when they called me on the cell phone I had left with them. Sorry I am not to have been here to greet you on your arrival but I have my little house trailer on the south side of Big Pine parked. It was nice of you to break a trail through the deep snow or I might have had more trouble getting here.

He said something to his men and one said, "Ja wohl, Herr Komandant and they stood at attention by the table. Herr Komandant continued then, "I am afraid I can not have you upsetting our plans any longer, Herr Thomas. I had hoped you would get me the money you owe us However I think your, so beautiful wife, will be more than anxious to handle this transaction when she knows that the safety of her little ones are at stake. I am afraid that you and your freund I must now shoot, then my men and I will track down the escaped hostages. In this weather, they cannot be far away. With my new plan, we will need them no longer. I regret that we must dispose of them also. War is Hell, is it not? Und now, Wilhelm, you do not mind if I call you, Wilhelm? You und your freund, outside. We will need this place a little while so

I must on the outside, shoot you. Verne preceded me out the door. I know we were both looking for an opportunity to do something but it did not look like we had one at the moment. Bruno had not cut his men loose yet as he knew, he must keep his eyes and gun on us. They stood in the doorway in their plastic restraints, watching.

We got about twenty feet out and Bruno had us halt. He told us to move over to the side away from the front of the building and raised his pistol. We must make our move, ***now***! Then all hell broke loose. When his men shouted something, Bruno whirled and shot. My gosh; he is quick! There stood Roberta and his shot had whirled her around and she had dropped the pistol she was pointing at him as she fell to the ground. His raised his pistol again and then, kaboom. kaboom. There is no mistaking the sound of a shotgun. Gretchen had risen from the snow only fifteen feet away and fired two shots from the twelve-gauge riot gun that had been in the jeep. Those just about cut Bruno in two; he never knew what hit him. Gretchen had a wintry little smile and muttered something in German

Roberta told me later that she had said she was avenging the death of her husband that he had killed. Now her dear Gustave could rest in peace. I remembered then the expression on the faces of Elke and Gretchen at the Tiergarten when they had heard that likely Bruno had been responsible for his death. Either one would have been happy to be the one to pull the trigger that ended the life of the one responsible for their Gustave's death. Strange, I had never heard his name even mentioned before now.

The kidnappers had thrown up their hands and were jabbering something until I guess Gretchen must have told them to shut up. Having one of your hostages suddenly show up with a shotgun she didn't mind shooting was likely somewhat unnerving. I ran inside to retrieve our guns and then ran to help carry Roberta inside. She told us it was her right arm that was hit. She was sorry to have been so slow. I told her, "Just you don't worry my dear; we will take care of you."

It was warm in the cabin now and we got her jacket and sweater off. You could see that the round had gone all the way through. It didn't appear any bones had been hit but there was quite a bit of bleeding. Roberta said it was now beginning to hurt like hell. Verne had brought in the first aid kit from the jeep. While I tried to stop the bleeding he got on the cell phone, ordered the helicopter in, and had them alert the hospital that we had a gunshot victim coming. I gave her four Tylenol tablets to try to ease the pain but held off on any aspirin. We didn't need to thin out her blood while we were trying to stop the bleeding.

While Gretchen held the compresses on Roberta, I went across the bridge into the meadow and waited to listen for the arrival of the helicopter. Verne had brought the jeep up to the cabin. When the helicopter was in, we could load Roberta into the jeep and have her at the helicopter in minutes. In fifteen minutes, I could hear the welcome sound of the helicopter rotor.

When it was a little closer, I turned on my flashlight and began waving it back and forth. When the pilot saw it, he turned on their big spot light then landing lights and came in for a landing. Verne was already there with the Jeep and with the help of the EMT on board, we soon had Roberta on board. The medic started work on her immediately. I told him she had only had the Tylenol. We put Gretchen on board as well. She looked pale and somewhat shaken. I don't think she had ever shot anyone and I told the medic why he should keep an eye on her and be sure she didn't go into shock. He told us not to worry. Everything would be taken care of. They should be at the hospital in minutes and, they were off.

Verne and I took the jeep back to the cabin and, what do you know, the prisoners had not run off. I really hadn't expected they would under the circumstances. We took the coffee and sandwiches inside and decided that we had now earned a little time to rest, and unwind. We built up the fire a little, got rid of the heavy jackets and sat the table with the sandwiches and coffee between us. Boy! Utter ambrosia! I needed that! We could see the prisoners were dying for something to eat. They looked like they had not eaten for a week.

Lucky for them we were not the same kind of people they apparently were. We each took another sandwich and pushed the rest over to them along with what coffee was still in one thermos. We kept the full thermos for ourselves. It could still be a long night. Boy did they ever gobble up the sandwiches, all the while saying, "Dahnke, dahnke." Verne had gotten busy in his cell phone, notifying his office we had a couple needing transportation and had them notify the coroner's office we had a job for him as well. He told them to find out where Agent Clarke was and notify him that the hostages were free and by now should be at the hospital. He can notify the CIA agents. It was now nine-thirty; we had started out about four o'clock. It had been a busy evening and it did not look like we were finished yet!

Chapter Twenty

WE HAD TO WAIT until a couple deputies 'coptered in and got the prisoners and then for a deputy coroner to come and collect Bruno. Thank goodness for helicopters! It was three AM when we finally drove the jeep into the Sheriff's Office parking lot. Someone from Mammoth would be by eventually to pick up the snowmobiles and Bruno's car. Except for someone repairing the lock to the cabin door and getting rid of the smoke smell, I guess we are finished. I said goodnight to any still at the office and headed for my nest. I shall most likely stay in bed about three days, barring, floods, tornadoes, earthquakes or possibly the smell of something really good cooking.

Well, I didn't actually stay in bed for three days although Grethel said I could if I wished. I didn't leap from bed at daybreak like a startled gazelle though either. About the third day I wandered down to the office to see if Verne had cut me loose and praise be, he had. Al had been by and interviewed the prisoners. They had agreed to plead guilty to the kidnapping charge in order to avoid the likelihood of a death sentence. If they ever get out they will be deported to Germany to await whatever that Government has in store for them. Al told Verne to let me know they also were through with my services; at least until they found some other nest of miscreants that needed my expert intervention. Very funny.

Gretchen was only in the hospital overnight. I guess the death of Bruno was some kind of closure for her. She seemed like a different person. Elvira/Elke also seemed now to be a different person. I hadn't realized how much the death of Gustave had weighed on them. Elvira says she is Elvira from now on. Forget that Elke had ever existed. Elaine came by to tell me she had located a small hotel for sale at a good price. Would I like to go and see it? I can see things are quickly getting back to normal.

Actually, I had been out looking at potential building sites. I had been out all afternoon and by the time I got home, I was pooped. Grethel said to go stretch out in the den and take a little nap. Gretchen had been helping out with *my* children all day and they had decided that maybe tonight we would have a little party.. Maybe invite Verne and Francine and Elaine, if she can get away from the Roadrunner. She would be sure and awaken me in time for me to get into my tuxedo. When she saw my startled expression, she laughed and said she had just wanted to see my startled expression. Sheesh----I never should have started kidding her. She is now worse than I ever was. That was what I was thinking as I fell asleep. I slept .like a log. Perhaps I may have previously mentioned, the salutary effects of an exceptionally clear conscience??

As I woke up, I thought I detected a familiar aroma. Could it be? I rushed out to the kitchen and there was Gretchen with a big smile on her face. "Ah, Wilhelm," she said when she saw me. "Maybe tonight you have the strength for mine red cabbage und sauerbraten to essen?" I grabbed her and gave her a big kiss and hug saying, "I have decide to divorce that woman I am married to, I can't recall her name at the moment, and marry you." She giggled. Grethel who was standing there said, "I expected something like this might happen. I have packed a small bag of necessities for you and it is standing ready for you by the front door when you have finished eating." Golly, Ned; I just can't win anymore. Is there just no respect any longer for the aged? When I asked, all I got was a gale of gay, girlish .laughter.

Now, was that ever a delicious meal! Verne wondered what we were having the next night and at what time. He did not want to be late. Gretchen was of course delighted that all her work had been so appreciated. Elaine suggested she might like to cook the same meal once a week or month at the Roadrunner. Gretchen said why did they not try it once first and see what happened, then they could talk.

CHAPTER TWENTY-ONE

WHAT A DIFFERENCE A day makes? Well a few weeks anyway. Gretchen now cooks at the Roadrunner once a week. The only thing on the menu that night is her sweet and sour red cabbage with Sauerbraten and potato pancakes. They had found out no one ever ordered anything else anyway. Reservations were a must for Sauerbraten Night. Gretchen has now become something of a minor celebrity here. Elvira is still packing in the young lads and wanna-bees. My favorite Bob, Roberta has almost recovered. She elected to stay in the hospital here instead of transferring to Walter-Reed as offered. Gretchen lives with us most of the time now, when she isn't cooking, and helps with the *humorous* offspring. Al Clarke will have completed twenty-five years of service with the FBI next year and says he will retire. He and Elaine will probably marry then. Our new house, complete with the clubhouse of the Loyal and Fraternal Order of Bobs, actually the den, will be ready in six months. Eschewing Elaine's advice, I decided not to buy a small hotel. I'm sure this house will prove to be quite adequate.

I guess that does it, except, I guess, for transferring the money in that numbered account in the Bank of Lichtenstein. How difficult can *that* be? It will only take a quick plane trip to Vaduz by way of Zurich or Berne; not more than three or four days total at the most. Shouldn't be any problem at all--------------------------should it?

Und now, mein Freunds,
das ist alles.

Danke,

***G**olly! **I** **T**hought **Y**ou **K**new; **I** **W**as **O**nly **K**idding!

Did you really think it was maybe something in Polish or perhaps Bulgarian? Now you know. Kinda surprised you didn't I??

I hope you liked my story. If so, there are more of them out there somewhere you might want to search out.